IMPULSIVE LOVE

LOVE STINGS SERIES #5

EVAN GRACE

LIMITLESS
PUBLISHING

Unexpected Love

Copyright © 2022 by Evan Grace.

All rights reserved.

First Print Edition: February 2022

Limitless Publishing, LLC

Kailua, HI 96734

www.limitlesspublishing.com

Formatting: Limitless Publishing

ISBN-13: 978-1-64034-632-1

My 37 year old cousin lost her battle with cancer. This book is dedicated to her.

HADDIE

I grab my Fundamentals of Nursing textbook, my notebook, and my laptop, stuffing them into my backpack. "Only six months left," I whisper to myself. Since my senior year of high school I've worked my butt off. First, it was taking all my prerequisites, and then it was starting nursing school.

Ever since I was a little girl I've known I wanted to be a nurse. Right now while I'm in nursing school, I work part-time as a hospice at home healthcare aide.

I go into homes and help with showering, bathing, and any other daily cares that they have trouble with themselves. I see patients who are in our hospice program, they're at the end of their lives and deserve to be treated with respect and dignity.

The manager for the hospice program said she'd hire me to be one of their nurses as soon as I graduated and passed my NCLEX. Hopefully I pass them on the first try. Doing hospice I get to meet so many wonderful people. Some I get to take care of for a long time, and some are only with us for a short time.

I get strange looks when people hear I'm in nursing school, and they hear the area that I want to work in, hospice. I'll hear people say, "Oh that'd be so sad." or, "how morbid." I've learned to ignore it.

I'm only able to work part-time while going to school, getting the bulk of my hours on the weekends, which means I don't have much of a life, not like I did much anyway. My parents help pay for my apartment even though I'd had quite a bit in savings when I moved out. They just didn't want me having the added stress—I'm the baby, they spoil me.

Don't get me wrong, I could afford this place on my own, but they didn't want me working all the time, and having it affect my studies.

I straighten up my little apartment, which thankfully takes no time at all. My dad was against me moving into my own place, which I get—my dad has always been overprotective of us girls.

My mom worked whatever magic she had on Dad, convincing him I was old enough and mature enough to live on my own. It could be possible that he didn't want me to leave because I was the last kid at home.

You'd think after raising four kids he'd want the quiet, but they're always having family dinners. The only one we usually miss is my brother, Parker. He's living in Charleston right now while he does his electrician apprenticeship. In his place we've got Chloe, Joe's wife. She's amazing and I love her for my brother.

She's pregnant with their second baby. She'd miscarried around twelve weeks the first time around, but this time she's almost to her due date. They're having a boy, but they aren't going to name him until he's born.

It seems to be babypalooza around here. My sister has four, my cousin Carrington has three, my cousin Violet has one. Soon Joe and Chloe will be adding one to the ever-growing brood. I'm not sure I want kids, but I'm only nineteen—almost twenty, I've got time to decide.

In the bathroom, I brush out my strawberry blonde curls and throw my hair up into a haphazard knot. I grab my toiletries and carry them into my room, tossing them into my duffle bag on top of the clothes I'm taking with me.

My sister's husband works for the police department and needs to work third shift the next couple of nights and I'm going to go stay with them to help Abby. The kids keep her crazy busy. They're good kids, but if I can help lighten the load, I will.

I carry my bag into the living room and set it by the door. With a quick look around, I make sure I've got everything. I throw my backpack over both of my shoulders, and grab my duffle bag. I step outside, it's still freaking hot out, and it's seven o'clock.

I shlep my bags to my tricked out candy apple red Toyota Corolla. I bought it off a friend of my brother-in-law's. The color was custom, the windows are tinted, it's got a sweet moonroof—I don't know about the engine, but it's really fast and purrs like a kitten.

I toss my bags in the backseat and shut the door.

"Haddie!" I close my eyes, sucking in a breath, and turn to fake smile at my neighbor, Lance. He can be irritating sometimes and constantly asks me out. "Where are you off to?"

I have to constantly go down to his apartment and tell him to turn his music down. I still haven't figured out what he does for a living. I know he works from home, and it's something with computers.

"I'm heading to my sister's." I open the driver's side door, "Well, it was good seeing you."

Lance grabs the top of my door—I freaking hate when he does this. "I'm having a party this weekend. Say you'll come."

Because I'm a glutton for punishment I always say yes,

and I always go. He's harmless, as are his friends. I shouldn't say it's punishment because I do enjoy myself, We're just very different and have nothing in common. "I'll try to make it, but you know I work every weekend."

He does a fist pump. "That's great. Everyone is going to be stoked to see you." Lance steps back from my door. "Tell Abby I said what's up?"

I nod, and give him a wave.

Reaching Abby's, I pull into the driveway next to Ben's cruiser. I climb out and then grab my bags. My niece, Natalie, opens the front door and comes running out to me.

"You're here." I drop my bags and pick her up. "I've missed you, Aunt Haddie."

"I've missed you too." I set her down and she tries to carry my book bag, which is heavy. I swap her and give her my duffle bag.

Inside the house is pure chaos—my nephews come tearing through the house. The boys, Rion and Dalton, are only a year apart. Princess Paisley tries to catch up with them until she sees me, and changes course.

"Pay pay." I squat down and she flings herself at me. She looks more and more like her big sister. They both have light tanned skin, hazel eyes, and light brown curls.

My sister comes out from the hallway followed by my brother in law. I won't lie, Ben is hot in his uniform. "Hey girlie." My sister wraps her arms around me. "Thanks for coming."

"Of course." I look at my brother-in-law, who pulls Abby away from me playfully, and wraps his arms around her. "Hey Ben." He lets go of his wife, and gives me a hug.

He takes his daughter from me, snuggling her close to his chest. Abby takes my duffel bag and disappears down the hall, and I take my book bag into living room.

Ben says goodbye to us and Abby follows him outside.

"Where are my two favorite boys?" I call. My nephews come running into the living room, tackling me to the floor. "The tickle monster is going to get you."

They both scream as I tickle them. When my sister comes in she just shakes her head and takes the baby into the back—probably to nurse her before bed.

"Okay, guys. I want you both to pick two books for me to read to you at bedtime." They disappear down the hall to their bedroom.

Natalie uses their absence as an opportunity to get some snuggle time. "The boys are driving me crazy."

I wrap my arm around her shoulders, hugging her into my side. "It won't be that way forever. I promise."

After story time and tucking in the older kids, I sit on the floor with Paisley lying across my lap, fast asleep. Abby's folding laundry and I'm calling my patients for tomorrow. My scheduler tells me I have a new hospice patient. As I listen to the information, the name sounds familiar, but I can't place it.

I only have three people to see and that takes no time at all.

I call the new patient first, a man answers. "Hello?" God, he sounds tired.

"Hi this is Haddie, the bath aide from the visiting nurses. Your wife Madison is on my schedule tomorrow." I open my mouth to speak, but he interrupts me.

"Haddie? Haddie Carmichael? You're Joe's sister."

"Uh…yes. I am. Do I know you?" I stroke my hand over Paisley's belly.

He clears his throat. "My son is Chris." I try not to roll my eyes because Chris is a mega douche. He and my brother were two peas in a manwhore pod until Joe met Chloe. The douche, on the other hand, will never change.

"Oh yes. I'm sorry, Mr. Anderson. How is Mrs. Anderson

doing?" Chris's parents are wealthy, but they've always been down to earth, always welcoming. They always invited all of us kids to Chris's parties when we were younger. I don't know how they raised such an a-hole.

"She's hanging in there. We've stopped chemo, and are just working on keeping her comfortable."

I couldn't imagine losing my mom or dad, heck I hate the thought of my grandparents getting older. "Will she feel uncomfortable having me help with her bathing tomorrow? I can have them send someone else."

"No, I'm kind of glad it's you. I think it'll make her more comfortable. She's lost so much weight she doesn't like me looking at her." His voice laced with sadness.

"Okay, I'll keep her feeling comfortable. I'd like to come at noon tomorrow, if that's okay. I'm in class in the morning." Abby comes back in from putting the laundry away and sits down, smiling at her daughter asleep on me.

"That sounds perfect. Thanks, Haddie."

"You bet, see you tomorrow, Mr. Anderson." I disconnect and call my other two patients, and once I get them scheduled, I toss my phone on my bag.

"I know you can't talk about it, but it's sad about Chris's mom. She's got pancreatic cancer and they caught it too late. They tried two rounds of chemo and then she said no more. I can't believe you didn't know that. Joe says Chris is not handling it well."

I pick up Paisley and snuggle her to my chest. "I'm sure that's not easy to deal with. I'll take this one to bed." I get up off the floor with her in my arms and carry her down the hall to the room she shares with her big sister. I lay her down and she rolls to her side. I shut the door and head back to the living room.

"Did she fuss at all?" Abby asks before taking a drink of her water.

"Nope, she was perfect." I pull out my textbook and study for a little bit before I start nodding off.

Abby locks up and we head to bed. I crawl into her bed with her following behind. We've slept together on and off since I was little—I know that sounds weird, and she's ten years older than me, but we've always been very, very close.

In the dark she rolls over to face me. "Tell me what's going on in your life." See…this is why we lay in bed together —late night heart to hearts.

"Umm…not much. I pretty much just have school and work. I don't really have a life." I sigh because I hate to admit it. "Lance invited me to a party at his apartment this weekend and I'm supposed to tell you hey."

"All that boy needs is a makeover and he'd be totally cute." His clothes are always big and baggy on his slim frame and his hair is wild and crazy, but we are strictly friends. Abby gets quiet for a second, and then she surprises me. "Are you still a virgin because of what happened to me?"

I was twelve when Abby had been sexually assaulted. She became a nightmare afterward; using drugs, sleeping around, and it ended the day she'd tried to kill herself. Dad and I had been upstairs when we heard glass breaking and her screaming.

I stopped having nightmares a long time ago, but for the longest time I remembered watching my dad kick the door in and then finding my sister barely conscious on the floor. I remember sobbing hysterically while Daddy had me call 9-1-1. He had to force his fingers down her throat to try and get her to vomit up the pills.

It took my sister a long time before she turned her life around, but she did. Now you'd never know looking at her that she had wanted to end it all at one point.

"It's not because of that…I promise. I've just been so focused on getting through high school, and immediately

7

starting college. Plus being around you and Ben, Cari and Damien, Vi and Diego, I know what I want in a man, and I won't settle for anything less."

Abby grabs my hand. "Don't ever settle. I don't think I tell you enough how much I love you. You've been there for me and for my family whenever we've needed you. You're the best auntie to your nieces and nephews."

"Stop, you're going to make me cry, and you know I don't like to show emotion." Which is only slightly true, I just don't like people to see me cry because people tend to think you're weak if you do.

She wraps her arm around me and kisses my cheek. "Love you."

"I love you too." It isn't long before I feel myself slip into a deep sleep.

CHRIS

I blink away the sleepy, booze-addled fog my brain is in. I'm pinned to the bed by two bodies, and honestly I couldn't fucking tell you who they are. All I know is that I went out for drinks last night, and that's it. Not smart, I know, but it's been a shitty fucking year.

I shake the two females awake. They both push themselves up, and the redhead tries to snuggle up to me. "No, babe, it's time for you guys to get gone. I've got shit to do." I climb out of bed, and see that I have a condom hanging from my dick. Fuck me, at least I was safe.

In the bathroom, I hop in the shower and scrub myself down with water so hot I can barely stand it. Then I turn the water to cold, letting it shock my system. Once I'm done, I wrap a towel around my waist and stop in front of the mirror. Fuck, I look tired. I grab some eye drops out of the medicine cabinet and squirt a couple of drops in each eye.

I brush my teeth twice to get rid of the taste of pussy, cigarettes, and whiskey. I use my electric razor to shave the stubble from my face—my mom likes it better when I'm clean shaven, and at this point I'll do anything to make her happy.

Just thinking about my mom makes my stomach turn. She's dying, and there's not a fucking thing I can do about it. When they told us the chemo didn't work and that we should put her into hospice, I'd hid in the bathroom and fucking bawled my eyes out.

At first I'd been in a state of denial, and then when anger set in I started getting drunk and high every fucking night, fucking anything with a pussy and a pulse. Last night was the last time I let that shit happen. It doesn't fucking help, and all it does is make me feel like shit. I've been such a disappointment to my folks. I honestly don't know how to make it right, and I'm running out of time to try.

At least my job has understood everything that's going on. They helped me fill out forms for FMLA, which protects my job when I need to be with my mom. I'm a realtor, so my job is already flexible. I didn't always want to be a realtor, but let's face it, I fucked around in high school, flunked out of college, and have no fucking skills. I at least was able to pass my real estate exam.

I've always used my good looks, my cock, and my parents' money to get what I wanted, and who I wanted. By the time I turned twenty-three, my parents finally had to give me the come to Jesus talk, and I finally pulled my head out of my ass and got my realtor's license.

I work for Hometown Realty, and for the past three years I've become one of their top agents. They all fucking love me, and more than one has tried to get into my bed, but that is one thing I don't do, fuck the women I work with. I did it once and it was the biggest fucking mistake ever.

I step back into my bedroom, and thankfully the girls are gone. Today someone is coming to help Mom with her bathing. It hurts knowing she's not strong enough to do it herself. She didn't want Dad or I doing it. I don't know why…maybe embarrassment.

I throw on a pair of basketball shorts and a sleeveless t-shirt. In my living room, I throw on my tennis shoes. I grab my phone, wallet, and keys, and head out to my black BMW X3.

My dad's already gone by the time I pull into their drive-way. He bought this house for my mom right after they got married. My dad comes from old money and it was the inheritance my grandfather left him. The same one is waiting for me. I get it when I turn thirty or get married, whichever comes first.

Dad owns his own law firm, but he's letting his associates take the bulk of the cases right now. Today he had a meeting, so I promised I'd be here for Mom's home care visit. I climb out of my car and look around. The lawn looks like shit. Mom usually was the one who called the lawn guy. Maybe when the person is here today I'll take care of the yard so my mom has something nice to look at.

I use my keys to let myself in. "Mom?"

"In the family room, baby." I head down the hall and find my mom curled up on the chaise lounge, some soap opera plays on the flat screen. She smiles when I step into the room. "Hi, handsome."

I bend down and kiss her cheek. "Are you feeling okay?" I sit down by her feet. "Any pain today?" She shakes her head.

I got my dark blond hair from her, but right now she's bald from the chemo. She wears scarves wrapped around her head to hide the hair loss. Mom's always been thin, but now she's scary thin. The pain in her stomach is the worst. She sometimes is in so much pain all she can do is lay there and cry.

The hospice nurse said they'd make sure the pain was

kept under control. "Are you hungry? I could make you some soup."

She smiles and grabs my hand—god, her hand feels cold and boney. "I'd love some soup, thank you." Mom stops me from getting up. "Did Dad tell you who's coming to help me get cleaned up?" I shake my head. "Haddie Carmichael."

"Joe's sister?" She nods. "Is she even old enough to be working? What is she, twelve?"

"Oh hush, she's not twelve." The doorbell rings. "Will you let her in?"

I make my way to the front door, and through the window I see her. She's fucking gorgeous; tall, willowy, the same gorgeous strawberry blonde hair, and light blue eyes—she can't be little Haddie Carmichael, but that's her. I open the front door.

"Hey Haddie, how are you?"

"I'm good, Chris." She leans in just enough so I can smell the light fruity scent of her. "I'm sorry about your mom."

"T-Thanks. Come on in. I was just getting ready to make her some soup. Should I wait?" I scrub a hand over my head.

"No, if she's hungry she should eat. I gave myself plenty of time here before my next patient."

I tell her Mom's in the family room and she follows me down the hall.

"Mom, look who's here."

Haddie steps into the room. "Hi, Mrs. Anderson. I don't know if you remember me, but I'm Joe's sister."

"Well, didn't you grow up to be a beauty, and please, call me Madison." Mom opens her arms and smiles as Haddie leans down to give her a hug.

I leave them to talk while I make Mom some soup. I pause because I hear Mom laughing, a sound I swore I'd never hear again, and it makes me smile.

Once the soup's done, I carry it out on a tray with her

meds. I find them sitting side by side and looking at Haddie's phone. "What are you guys doing?"

My mom smiles up at me. "Haddie was just showing me pictures of Abby's children. They're all so beautiful." She turns to Haddie. "I finally met Joe's wife. She sure is pretty and he seems so happy."

"She's great, and they just found out they're having a boy."

Mom looks at me. "Did you know that, Chris? I'll have to get online and get them a gift." Joe's wife does not like me, not that I can blame her. When they came to a party here I said some things to her that I'm not proud of.

Joe and I are still friends, but these days we don't see each other much. He's all domesticated now—I'm happy for him, but I'm clearly not in a relationship and don't really plan on it. Maybe one day Chloe will forgive me for being a douche, but I'm not holding my breath.

After Mom eats her soup, Haddie helps her stand, bends to grab her bag, and disappears down the hall with her.

I rinse off the dishes, stick them in the dishwasher, and then head outside. I find the riding lawnmower in the shed, and push it out into the yard. After I gas it up, I climb on and start it up—I can't remember the last time I did this—junior high…maybe? How pathetic is that?

It takes me a good half hour to finish, and after I put the riding mower away, I run inside to check on Mom. I step into my parents' bedroom and put my ear to the door. The shower is running and I can hear their voices muffled through the door.

I head back outside and grab the weed whacker, and work on the edges of the lawn. By the time I'm done my shirt is sopping wet. I pull it off and toss it on the railing of the deck, but I'm proud, because when I look around, the yard actually looks pretty good. After locking the shed up, I turn around finding Haddie standing on the steps.

I don't miss her eyes on my bare chest, or the way her cheeks turn pink, but she quickly looks away. "I'm all finished with your mom. She was worn out by the time we finished and she's lying down. I'll be back on Wednesday."

Haddie disappears around the side of the house. I shouldn't follow her, but that doesn't stop me from doing it. She's already throwing her bag in her car when I reach her. "Wait up." Haddie stops and turns to me. "Thanks for being so good with her. This has been so hard on her."

Her eyes soften as she walks toward me. "I hate this for your family. She's always treated my family with such kindness."

"It's pancreatic." She nods. I know she's in nursing school, so she's got to know how bad that is. "Yeah, she did two rounds of chemo, but decided she wasn't going to spend the rest of her time sick. It's comfort measures only."

Haddie nods. "Can't say I blame her." She looks at her watch. "I really need to get going to my next patient. It was good seeing you, Chris." She climbs into her car and I watch her back out of the driveway.

* * *

I SHRUG into my black fitted suit jacket and step in front of the mirror, straightening the collar of my white dress shirt. I look closely and don't miss the lines around my eyes. I'm twenty-six years old, but today I feel so much older.

My body aches, my head hurts, and I've got the fucking shakes. I know why, I haven't drank in a week, or done any other illegal substance. I'm having fucking withdrawals and it scares me, but I'm trying to power through it.

Yesterday I went to the pharmacy and got myself some vitamins and a cleanse to hopefully get myself through this.

In the bathroom I grab the bottle of ibuprofen and shake a couple pills into my hand, then pop them in my mouth.

I run my hands through my dark blond hair. It's over a month past due for a cut, but it's so far down on my priority list. Instead I add a little wax, rubbing it through my hair until its slicked back enough that's it's not hanging in my face.

In my kitchen I grab the file for the property I'm showing today. It's a horse farm with the land sitting right off the marshes of the Atlantic Ocean. The owners never had children to pass it down to and are moving to Florida.

The husband kept the property in good shape even though it's been a few years since they had any horses. The couple looking to buy are in their thirties with little kids. The husband breeds Arabians.

If I make this sale I could make a thirty thousand dollar commission. It'll be my most expensive property to date, and I fucking need this right now. I shove my wallet into my back pocket and put my silver aviators on.

On my way to the property, I stop by Starbucks and pick up an iced coffee and a muffin. By the time I reach the property I've devoured it and guzzled my coffee. I hold out my hand and see that the trembling has stopped—for now, thank fuck.

I pull into the driveway and see that I've beat them here. I let myself in and do a quick walk through to make sure nobody else is in here and that nothing is out of place. Back downstairs, I grab the contract and make sure everything is in there. I pop an Altoid in my mouth just as the sound of a car pulling up draws my attention toward the front.

I stop at the mirror in the hall and straighten my jacket before stepping outside and give the Danielson family a wave.

By the time we're done with the walkthrough, their realtor is telling me their offer, which my client accepts—they'd already given me a price range that they approved. They have the earnest money with them, and after I take it I have them sign the contract. My clients wanted to get this over with as soon as possible, which is why they agreed to a short closing period.

Once they leave, I head into the house and give a fist pump and a shout. I pull out my phone and call my mom. She sounds so tired when she answers. "Hi, my baby boy. How did it go?"

My eyes burn and I pinch the bridge of my nose. I clear my throat. "I sold it."

"You did? That's so great. Are you going to go out and celebrate?" Normally that's exactly what I'd do—buy a bottle of Macallan single malt, maybe do some coke, and have a lady or two keep me company for the night.

"I thought I'd bring over some Chinese and have dinner with you guys."

"Are you sure?" Just the happiness in her voice makes me glad I'm doing this—an ache fills my gut because I know I won't have her much longer.

"Absolutely, there's no one I'd rather celebrate with. I'll get you some of your egg drop soup and some rice and vegetables, how about that?" She's lost her appetite and somedays it's a struggle for her to eat at least once a day. My mom's oncologist said to supplement with protein shakes, so I bought her one of those Ninja blenders and a recipe book of smoothie recipes.

"That sounds really good." I hear her yawn.

"I'll be over around six. Get some sleep. I love you."

"I love you too."

I hang up, then lock up the house before heading to the office and getting the paperwork filed. A couple of the other realtors stop by to congratulate me on the sale. My secretary,

Jane, ran to the bakery down the street and picked me up a congratulatory cupcake and had it waiting on my desk when I got back. She's old enough to be my grandma, but she keeps me in line.

Ducking out of the office a little early, I head home and change into shorts and a t-shirt. I stop at China Dragon to pick up dinner. I order at the counter and then sit down at a table by the door. My eyes scan the restaurant and I see Joe sitting at a booth in the back with his wife.

I should leave them alone since she hates me, but against my better judgment I get up and walk toward their table.

Joe smiles when he sees me. "What's up, brother?" We give each other a back slapping hug. I pull back and smile down at Chloe as I sit down. "Hey Chloe."

"How are you? How's your mom?" Our parents have been like second parents to each other since we met in grade school.

"She's okay. Just walking through the house wears her out. Luckily now that she's in hospice, the nurses come to her. Your sister is her aide. She helps her get cleaned up, but mainly just sits and talks to her." I don't miss the way Joe's chest puffs with pride.

I'm surprised when Chloe talks to me. "Haddie's going to make a wonderful nurse. If you ever need someone to sit with your mom or anything, I'd love to help." What's more shocking is she reaches out and grabs my hand.

"Thanks, I appreciate that." Her smile is genuine, at least the first genuine smile I've ever received from her. The hostess brings me my food. I stand up. "Have a good rest of your night."

"Call me and we'll meet for lunch or a game of one on one so I can kick your ass." We always go to his parents' place since they have a basketball hoop. He stands and pulls me into a bear hug. "Anything you need, brother. I mean it."

"Thanks." I pound his back and then clasp him on his shoulder, giving it a squeeze. I smile down at Chloe. "Take care and keep this one in line."

I make my way toward my childhood home and pull into the driveway behind my dad's car. For a moment I just sit and stare at the front of the house. What are we going to do without her? She's always been there, always the room mother who was at every school function. She came and cheered me on at every sporting event, and made me my favorite meal and cake for my birthday. She did the same for my dad—always taking care of her men.

I take a deep breath and shake out my hands, the damn things are starting to tremble again—only this time it's from holding in the sadness and anger that I feel.

Inside I hear the TV and then Mom's soft laughter. "Who's hungry?" I step into the family room and both of my parents turn to smile at me.

"Thanks for bringing dinner, son." It's still surprising that my parents even still speak to me after all the grief I've caused them over the years, but they love me unconditionally. I'm pretty sure my mom qualifies for sainthood at this point.

He grabs the plates and silverware while I pull the containers from the bag. "Look at my boys working side by side," Mom says, walking toward the counter.

I smile at her and can't help but notice how pale she is. I pour her soup into a bowl and set it on the island in front of her. We both join her and the three of us eat together for the first time in a long time.

After dinner, Mom zonks out on the chaise lounge watching some sitcom and Dad signals for me to come outside with him. He pulls out two cigars and hands me one. We light them and I wait patiently for my dad to say whatever he has to say.

"I wake up every morning and the first thing I do is make sure she's breathing. How am I supposed to go on without her?" I don't respond because I don't have the answer. "I've been with your mom since I was eighteen years old. The minute I laid eyes on her I knew she was it for me." Neither of us says anything for a long time.

Dad finally says, "Thank you for coming over tonight." I nod because my response is stuck in my throat. I take a puff of my cigar and blow smoke rings. My dad turns to me. "Your mom says you made a big sale today."

"Yeah, a horse farm. I sold it for two million nine."

"That's great, son. I'm so proud of you. It took you a while to find your path, but I'm glad you did."

We puff our cigars and take in the night. I can't remember the last time my dad told me he was proud of me, but I'll take it.

HADDIE

I close my psychiatric-mental health nursing textbook and shove it in my backpack along with my notebook. I stand up and stretch. Putting my backpack on, I step out into the hall. This course has been hard on me —maybe because of what happened with my sister.

To this day I remember what it was like to sit in that room across from Abby and have to tell her what it felt like to find her on her floor. To have to call 9-1-1 and watch them load her onto the gurney.

The mental trauma took a long time to go away, but she worked hard to overcome it. We all did.

I shake off those thoughts and head down the hall toward the doors.

"Hey you." I turn to find a guy walking toward me. I've never seen him before because he's so hot that I'm sure I'd remember him. His dark hair is back in one of those man buns and he's got the greenest eyes I've ever seen.

"Yes?" He keeps walking until he's a foot away from me. "Did you need something?"

"I'm Graham. I haven't seen you around here before."

Oh God, is this guy for real? I roll my eyes. "Yeah, I'm not interested." I start heading toward the door. His footsteps sound behind me, but I keep moving. "Why are you following me?" I say, not even looking behind me.

"Why won't you stop and talk to me?" He catches up to me. I sigh and stop, looking at him. "I don't mean any harm, seriously. You're just so pretty and I can't believe I haven't seen you before." He looks at me closely. "Fuck, I can tell I'm weirding you out. I'm sorry."

I shrug. "It's okay. I'm Haddie."

He smiles at me and he's got a great one; perfect straight, pearly whites. "Nice to meet you, Haddie. What are you studying?"

"I'm studying to be a nurse. How about you?" God, I suck at small talk.

"I'm doing the transfer program before going into criminal justice. I want to be a police officer."

"My brother and brother-in-law are both cops, and my cousin's husband is a detective." I can't help but smile because I'm so proud of them and all the good work they do. "My brother was actually shot while on duty, but he's doing so much better now."

We walk side by side toward the parking lot. I have no experience in this department whatsoever. I just keep watching him out of the corner of my eye. We reach my car, and I don't miss the appreciative look he gives it.

"Nice ride."

"Thanks. My brother-in-law found it for me. One of his friends was selling it." I grab my phone out of my pocket and see that I need to get going. "I'm meeting my parents for lunch, but it was nice meeting you, Graham."

"Nice meeting you too, Haddie." He stays on the sidewalk while I pull out of my space.

Ten minutes later I turn into the parking lot of The

Waterfront, a restaurant my family has frequented for as long as I can remember. I park next to my dad's truck and climb out of my car. Inside, I spot my parents sitting in front of the window. My dad sees me first and smiles widely before standing up.

"There's my girl." I step into his open arms. He kisses the top of my head before letting me go so I can hug my mom

The family joke is that I was switched at birth—it's the family joke because I look like none of my siblings or my parents. My mom is five foot two or three, like my sister. They're both blonde with cornflower blue eyes and have curves.

My dad is six three with dark hair and deep blue eyes. Joe could be his younger twin. My brother, Parker, is tall and leaner built. His hair is a lighter brown and has the same eye color as Mom.

I'm five feet ten with curly strawberry blonde hair. I'm what people call willowy, or as I like to call it, built like a boy. The only similarities I have are blue eyes like my mom's and have a tiny gap between my two front teeth like she does.

My brothers used to love telling me that dad found me at one of his work sites—assholes. "Hey Mom."

My dad pulls out my chair for me and has me sit right next to him.

"How was class?" my mom asks from across the table. She's been my biggest supporter since I told her I wanted to be a nurse.

"It was good, and thankfully this semester is almost over." I smile at them both. "Six months left."

Dad wraps his arm around my shoulders and hugs me into his side. My family is loud and crazy at times, but I wouldn't have it any other way. I'm so lucky because so many of my friends or acquaintances have parents who are divorced—not my parents. They've been through a lot and sometimes they fight, but they also love each other fiercely.

"We're so proud of you baby girl." My dad kisses my temple.

Our waitress brings our salads, and when I look up I see Chris sitting across the room staring in my direction. I raise my hand and give him a wave. He does the typical chin lift, my mom notices me looking and turns and gives Chris a wave.

"I feel so bad for them. I brought Madison lunch yesterday and she says you've been taking good care of her." Her smile is sad.

I don't tell her that every time I come to help her, Madison looks more and more sick. I also don't share that sometimes when I sleep I dream that it's Mom who's sick, and I wake up crying. That doesn't stop me from still wanting to do hospice care.

We eat our salads in a comfortable silence, but my eyes keep drifting to Chris. Every time I look at him he's looking at me. I can't name the look on his face except maybe a look of curiosity.

"Parker's coming home next weekend. We're planning a big party for him at the house." My mom isn't fully happy unless all her babies are home.

"That's great. Are Uncle Cash and Aunt Tessa coming with the kids?" Parker is living with our aunt and uncle in Charleston while he does his apprenticeship.

"I think they're going to come and stay Saturday night. The only one who can't come is Josie, but that's because she just started her new traveling gig in Atlanta."

Josie is the daughter of my aunt Tessa's brother, Jonathon. She's always come to visit with our aunt and uncle, and we love seeing her.

"That's too bad. I should call her and check in. Let me

know if you need me to bring anything." I don't cook much, but I've got a couple recipes that are my specialties. I make insane chocolate and salted caramel brownies. My dad has had me make them for him for his past two birthdays.

I excuse myself and head toward the back to go to the bathroom. Once I'm done, I wash my hands. Opening the door, I'm shocked to find Chris leaning against the wall. "Uh...hey. How are you?" He hasn't been at his parents' house the last couple of times I've been there.

"I'm good, I just wanted to say hi before I head back to the office. Uh...so, hi." Chris turns and then he's gone.

I shake my head. "That was weird."

I head back to the table and sit down, casually looking in the direction of where Chris is sitting and find them leaving. Shrugging off the disappointment I feel, I turn back and focus on my parents.

"I heard that Violet and Diego are moving here. Are they going to work with you?" My cousin and her husband are both architects...well, Violet has to finish school, which got delayed due to the birth of their daughter Lucy.

My dad nods. "Yep, when they get here we're going to expand the business. Your aunt's happy to have both of her babies home. I think Diego will bring a lot of fresh ideas to the table. The man knows his shit, that's for sure."

After we finish I head home. I don't have to work today, so I'll take a little nap and then get up to do my homework and study. I wave at my parents as they pull out, and then do the same.

* * *

I KNOCK before opening the door, announcing myself. "Mrs. Jensen, it's me, Haddie from visiting nurses."

She comes out, moving slowly with the assistance of her

walker. I've been seeing her for the past year. We help manage her congestive heart failure. "Hi Haddie, I'm sorry it's such a mess in here. I get so tired trying to pick up." Mrs. Jensen says the same thing to me every time, but I don't mind.

Her home is actually really clean, but I know that's because her granddaughter comes and cleans it once a week. I only see her once a week to help her get cleaned up and then tomorrow she'll get her hair done.

She tells me all of the latest gossip from the halls of the assisted living. Since I've been seeing her I know the entire scoop about everyone. I know who has dated whom and who doesn't get along.

Mrs. Jensen has got to be my favorite patient. It doesn't matter what kind of day I'm having, because when I'm here she makes me laugh and smile and I leave feeling happy. Today is no different and as I say goodbye, she's getting ready to go play bingo.

I have some time between patients, so I decided to stop at Starbucks and get an iced coffee. While I stand at the end of the counter, I glance around the shop. This place is always crowded, and there is never anywhere to sit.

In the corner I spot a familiar face. Turning to walk over to him, I think better of it when I spot Chris being Chris, heavily flirting with a leggy brunette. Her hand is on his chest and Chris's hand is on her thigh. I turn back to the counter, ignoring the weird ache in my gut. What the hell is wrong with me? I know what he's like. I've heard enough stories about Chris and my brother to last a lifetime. At least Joe is no longer like that. He's got Chloe, and is in love with his wife.

"Haddie." I step up to the counter and grab my drink. As I head to the exit, I resist the urge to look in Chris's direction, but at the last minute I fail...miserably. I turn and catch a glimpse of him leaning in close, talking to the woman who is clearly more his type than I am. Ugh…why do I even care?

I make my way out to my car. Maybe if I see Graham again and he asks me out, I'll say yes, and on that thought, I head to my last patient's home.

My patient is easy and I'm in and out of there in a half hour. "See you next week, Mr. Roberts."

"Yeah, yeah, yeah," he grumbles from his recliner.

Mr. Roberts doesn't see it, but when I open the door and step outside I'm smiling. He's a grumpy Gus, but I know he loves me. He'll refuse anyone else if they try to put him on someone else's schedule.

I head toward my sister and Ben's home—they've got a parent/teacher conference for Natalie and I volunteered to look after the other kiddos. Of course I am their favorite auntie. Oh, Ben's sisters are great, but they have families of their own, so it's much easier for me to watch them. I pull up in front of their house and then climb out of my car.

As the front door opens, I grab my backpack, and when I come around I'm hit by the sweetest little girl in the entire world. "Aunt Haddie." She hugs me around my waist and gives me a squeeze.

I stroke a hand over her tawny braids. "How's my girl? Are Mom and Dad going to get a good report on you today?"

She steps back and places her hand on her hip. "Well duhh!" Natalie struts back to the house with me chuckling as I follow behind her. They are going to have their hands full with her. I step inside and find Paisley crawling on top of her dad, who's lying on the floor.

Paisley squeals when she sees me so I pluck her right up from the floor, kissing her chubby cheeks. "What's up, bro?"

Ben gets up and gives me a hug, and a kiss on top of my head. Abby is seriously lucky, her husband is so sweet and freaking hot. "Thanks for coming and watching the monster crew."

"Any time." I hand Paisley back to her dad and find Abby and the boys painting at the table. "Hey guys." The boys both turn to me, smiling, sliding out of their seats. They come running toward me so I squat down and open my arms.

They're little brutes already and knock me on my ass. I cover them with smooches until they squeal. I watch Rion and Dalton run into the backyard and start wrestling. Abby comes over, holding out her hand to me and helping me up. I look her over and notice she's gotten skinny.

"What's up with you being all skinny? Why haven't I noticed this before?" Oh god, what if she's sick?

Abby grabs my biceps. "I can see the nurse wheels spinning. I'm fine, I wanted to start working out since we're done having babies, and a friend of Ben's owns a Crossfit box, so that's what I've been doing." She flexes and that's when I see she's cut.

"Holy shit, maybe I ought to join and do it with you." I've always been skinny and no matter how much I eat, I don't gain weight—it's a blessing and a curse. It's a blessing because I can satisfy my sweet tooth whenever I want without feeling guilty. It's a curse because I'm built like a boy and am constantly being told I should eat more, even though I do, a lot.

"Come with me tomorrow. Mom's watching the kids so I can go since Ben's working." We make plans and I follow her inside.

"Natalie, get your shoes on," Abby tells her before disappearing down the hall.

They leave a few minutes later and I sit down on the floor with Paisley while the boys disappear down the hall to their room to play. My sweet little niece crawls onto my lap. I grab my phone and take a selfie of us and then post it to Instagram with the hashtag baby love.

Not even two seconds later a CAnderson69 likes my photo. "Who is CAnderson, Paisley?" She grabs my phone, trying to put it in her mouth. "Um...no, little girl." After screeching at me, she grabs her baby doll and rocks it. I can only shake my head.

I pull up the profile and see that it's Chris—since when is he following me on Instagram? I scroll through his pictures —in half of them he's surrounded by beautiful women. Women with curves, big breasts, and skimpy clothing hang on him like he's the king of the world...barf.

I barely see Chris and all of a sudden I can't seem to get away from him everywhere I go. "Let's go check on your brothers." Paisley holds her arms up to me. I scoop her up and carry her down the hall to the boys' room. We find them playing trucks—well, it is more like demolition derby.

"Aunt Haddie, I want a snack." Dalton drops his truck and runs past me with Rion following close behind. Double trouble is what I like to call them. I don't know how my sister does it. They jump from one thing to another. I look down at Paisley. "I guess we should get a snack." She gives me a slobbery, toothy grin, and then goes into a baby babble tirade.

They haven't eaten dinner yet, so I get them set up with some grapes and animal crackers after sticking Paisley in her highchair. While they eat, I pull out my notes for my mental health nursing class. We've got a quiz on Friday and I want to be prepared.

Ben, Abby, and Natalie return home a half hour later, and of course my niece is getting excellent marks and her teacher loves her. After giving her snuggles, I decline their invitation to stay for dinner. I love them all, but I'm obviously not going to get any studying done here.

Abby walks me out to my car. "Thanks again for sitting with the kids."

"You do not need to thank me. I love spending time with them." I open the passenger side door and toss my backpack inside.

She sighs. "I know you love it, but sometimes I feel like I take advantage of you."

I can't help it and start to laugh. "You seriously think you take a-advantage of me." I wipe the tear from my eyes and get control of myself. "I love you. I love your husband, and I love those rowdy heathens you call your children. I'd do anything for you—for them."

Abby kisses my cheek and then hugs me tight. "I love you. Oh do you want to go with me tomorrow?"

I'm not what you'd call athletic—oh sure, when I was younger I danced, but I've never done sports. I'd only run if someone was chasing me. Of course I do like the idea of spending some uninterrupted time with my sister, who is my best friend. "Yeah okay, but you're responsible for getting my carcass home."

The butthead laughs. "You've got it."

* * *

"I THINK I'M DYING," I whimper from my spot on the floor.

It's official, I hate my sister. She's a big meanie, and I'm never speaking to her again.

Earlier she picked me up, and as soon as I saw Abby in her little bootie shorts and sports bra, I was immediately jealous. She's had three kids (Natalie is her adopted daughter) and is lean and tight where she should be.

She brought me a pair of her bootie shorts and a sports bra tank top—Abby's such a mom—and brought me a bottle of water too. When we got here, I was immediately intimidated by all the ripped men and women. First, I had to sign a release, and then Abby introduced me to a couple of her friends.

After that I don't remember anything, which brings me to now. I'm face down on a mat in the corner and my bitchface sister is laughing hysterically at me. I'm a sweaty, stinky mess right now, but I can't drum up enough energy to care.

"Come on, Haddie. You can't stay here all day."

I open my eyes to see her lying on the floor looking at me. Instead of answering, I hold up my hand and give her the finger. She stands up and holds her hand out to me. I let her pull me up until I'm standing. I feel like a newborn foal and my legs feel all jiggly.

It's not lost on me that Abby's Crossfit buddies are all laughing at me as we walk by. "I seriously hate your guts," I tell her as we step outside.

After Abby drops me off, I take a long hot bath in a tub filled with Epsom salts. When I climb out of my tub, I wrap a towel around myself and grab my bottle of ibuprofen. After swallowing them down I change into something comfy and crawl into my bed to promptly pass out.

CHRIS

*T*he club is loud and the girls may be hot, but I'm just not feeling it.

When some buddies had invited me out I thought it would be a good idea. Have some drinks, maybe get my dick sucked, and blow off some steam. Now that I'm here I've declined a drink, and I'm just not in the mood for any female companionship. I duck out early and text my dad.

Chris: Are you up?

It takes a minute before the dots start bouncing.

Dad: I am.

Chris: Is it okay if I come over?

Dad: Of course, you don't ever need to ask. I'm not sure how I got so lucky to have parents that still love me even though I've been a major asshole and disappointment to them.

I make my way across town and pull onto my parents' street. As a kid I terrorized this neighborhood; fucking shit up and acting like my shit didn't stink. Hell, I was like that at school too. I got the best-looking girls, I played every sport even though I wasn't that great, when I tried, I got good grades, and none of that shit means a damn thing now.

I blow out a breath as I pull into my parents' driveway. My dad will know something's up, and I can't let him see me like that. He's got more important shit to deal with. Speaking of my dad, he opens the front door as I shut my car off.

"Hi, son. What brings you by?"

I follow him inside. "I was out with some friends and just didn't feel like hanging out with them anymore. How's Mom?"

"She's been sleeping most of the day. Her stomach has been bothering her." My eyes burn, knowing the end is inevitable. I follow him into the kitchen and he grabs two beers out of the refrigerator. I take one, twisting the cap off. "This next week I have a meeting in Atlanta that I have to go to. I'll only be gone a day and half and I'm flying so it won't take me long to get back. I spoke to Haddie and she's going to stay here and take care of your mom. If you could stop by and check in on them that would be good."

"I can definitely do that."

I finish my beer and go look in on Mom. Her color is concerning and her breathing seems slightly off. My dad puts his hand on my shoulder. "She's okay, I promise." I know he's lying to me, but honestly I appreciate it right now.

We step back into the hall. "Is it okay if I stay here tonight?" I just don't feel like I should leave.

"Of course. You can sleep in your old room, one of the guest rooms, or the couch." He grabs me a spare toothbrush and I head into my old room. I don't have any clothes with me, so after brushing my teeth I strip down to my boxer briefs. I put my hands behind my head and stare up at the ceiling.

I glance out the window and see the moon shining bright. I close my eyes and make a wish, say a prayer, and beg for my mom to be spared. I'm not sure how long I lay here staring out the window before I finally feel exhaustion claim me.

* * *

I GRAB my duffle bag out of the backseat of my car and walk past Haddie's car as I head to the front door. I use my key to let myself in and drop my bag in the foyer. "Haddie?" I call out.

I listen intently and hear a muffled voice call out in the family room. Once I reach them I stop in the doorway. Mom is sitting up with Haddie right next to her. They're watching something on an iPad.

Mom looks up and smiles at me. "Come look, we're watching a video of all Abby's babies."

Haddie smiles, her cheeks turning a light shade of pink. Her pale blue eyes sparkle as she looks up at me. The gap between her two front teeth is unique, but fucking works on her. She's the only redhead I know who ever has a real tan, not the spray shit. Haddie is fucking gorgeous—how have I never noticed before? Oh, I know why—because she's my best friend's baby sister and too fucking young.

I mentally brush those thoughts away and sit down on my mom's other side. I watch the video and it's all of the babies of the Carmichael family. They're all running around the backyard. The kids are running around in circles, chasing each other with various sizes of water guns.

Haddie comes into view with a giant super soaker, chasing the kids around, spraying them. I notice Mom's hands trembling. Haddie grabs the iPad from her. "Madison, are you okay?"

She looks at me with tears starting to slide down her gaunt grey cheeks. "I'm nev-never going to be a g-grandma." Mom asks Haddie to help her back to the bedroom.

"I'm so sorry, Madison. I didn't mean to upset you," she says as she wraps her arm around my Mom's waist.

"No, no, honey. It's not your fault. I guess I just didn't want to think about that stuff before." I follow behind them as they walk through the house to the hallway where my parents' bedroom sits. Haddie gets Mom settled in bed.

I move to the bed and sit down next to her hip and grab her hand in mine. "Come on, Mom you know me. I'm too much of a Casanova to have babies." I give her my cockiest smirk.

She gives me a watery laugh. "Oh honey, you just haven't met the right woman yet, but you will."

Mom falls asleep pretty fast, which is the norm these days. Haddie turns on a little monitor and shows me what looks like a walkie talkie. "I'll be able to hear her if she gets up."

We walk silently side by side back to the family room. Before I sit down, Haddie grabs my forearm. "I didn't mean to upset your mom. I just thought it might make her smile."

"It's seriously okay. She knows you didn't mean any harm." I can see her eyes are starting to fill with unshed tears. Without a second thought I pull her into my arms. The moment she wraps her arms around my waist things just feel right. Instead of thinking about it, I choose to ignore it.

I ignore the fact that her hair smells like raspberries or that her willowy body fits perfectly against mine. Instead I let her go. "Are you hungry?" She nods, so I lead her to the kitchen and have her sit at the breakfast bar. "How's school? You're going for nursing, right?"

Haddie's eyes widen—I'm sure out of surprise because I'm a selfish dick. "Um…yeah. I only have six months left. Hospice is what I want to do."

"You'll make a good nurse. You take really good care of my mom."

I make us a couple of sandwiches and grab a bag of chips, setting it in between us. We eat quietly side by side. When we finish, I clean up the mess and she pulls out her textbooks and notebook. I leave her as she starts scribbling stuff on her pad of paper.

I'm a ball of nervous energy, and instead of staring at my mom while she sleeps, I go into the weight room and start lifting. Thankfully Haddie leaves me alone. I work myself into exhaustion, and when I finish, I head into my bathroom and shower—after, I throw on a pair of basketball shorts and a t-shirt then step into the hall, where I find Haddie stepping out of my parents' bedroom.

"Is my mom okay?" Can she see the worry on my face?

She stops in front of me, again resting her hand on my forearm. A strange tingling sensation travels up my arm. What is she doing to me?

"Your mom's fine. She's sleeping. Your dad texted me, asking me how she was. He got an earlier flight and should be home by eleven."

Should it bother me that my dad talked to Haddie about Mom? My phone rings, interrupting my thoughts. I head into the kitchen and grab my phone off of the counter. It's my dad. "Hey Dad, how's it going?"

"Good, son, we're finishing up ahead of schedule. Haddie says you're at the house."

"Yeah, I took today off and came to help in your absence."

"That's great. I'm sure your mom is glad to have you there." I hear him sigh. "Your mom and I updated our life insurance policies. You're the primary benefactor."

I interrupt him. "Dad, I really don't want to talk about this right now."

"Christopher, I know you don't, but let's face it. Your mom doesn't have much time left and you never know when my time is up. We want to ensure that you're taken care of. In

35

the safe in my office is the information for your mom if she p-passes before I get home. It's the mortuary, and the number. They already have the outfit she wants to be buried in." He swallowed hard.

"I'll call you when my flight lands, but you call me if anything changes with your mom."

"Yeah, Dad, I'll call you. I love you." I feel sick.

"I love you too, son."

As soon as I hang up, I drop my phone on the counter and grip the edge. My eyes and nose burn and I want to fucking cry. I feel arms wrap around me from the side. I don't even think, I just wrap my arms around her, hugging her to my chest. "This sucks so fucking bad."

"I'm so sorry, Chris. I wish there was something I could say or do that could help ease some of your pain."

She's only a few inches shorter than me, so I rest my cheek against her temple. "Thank you. Sometimes I think this is all a bad dream and I'll wake up and she'll be fine, but then I see her and realize it's not. Fuck, I can't take anymore sad right now. Do you want to watch a movie?"

"A movie sounds great." Her minty breath tickles my cheek.

I pull back and she looks at me with those big blue eyes of hers. My heart starts beating faster in my chest. The urge to kiss her takes over, but I resist it the best I can. "Um...come on. That's see what we can find." I let go of her and walk into the family room with her following slowly behind me.

We decide to watch *Step Brothers*, but as funny as I find that movie, I don't feel much like laughing. We're both silent as we watch. The sound of someone getting sick has both Haddie and I jumping up and running down the hall toward my parents' bedroom.

Haddie enters first and I freeze the moment I cross the threshold. Mom is on her side her gaunt cheek resting in a pool of her own vomit. I come unstuck and move toward the bed and watch Haddie kick into action.

She helps her sit up and talks softly to her. "Do you want to take a shower or do you want to just change and wash you up?"

"I'm so tired. Can we just wash me up?"

"Of course. Whatever you want." Haddie looks at me. "Can you change the sheets? I'll wash them once we're done."

I step in front of Mom and help stand her up while Haddie grabs her a clean nightgown. I help get them set up in the bathroom and do as Haddie asked and strip the bed. I get the fresh sheets and quickly throw them on, tucking in the ends.

When they come back out I've got Mom's bed ready for her. She smiles at me as they get close to the bed. I try to give her a smile, but I'm sure it looks fake, or at the very least, forced. Mom and Haddie stop right in front of me. My mom reaches up and cups my cheek. "You look just like your dad when we met. So handsome." She always says that, but I know it's her that I look like.

I place my hand over hers and ignore how boney and cold it feels. We get her in bed and she immediately falls asleep. I don't move from my spot next to the bed. It's like I'm afraid to leave her.

I feel Haddie get close to me, grabbing my hand in hers. She leans in close. "We can move the chaise lounge in here. Then we can keep an eye on her."

How was she able to read my thoughts?

Together we carry it into the room and place against the wall. I move the lamp and side table next to it so we can read or whatever. It ends up that Haddie curls up with her school-books and I play games and answer emails on my phone.

I'm not sure how much time passes before Haddie starts yawning. She shoves her books back in her bag. I wrap my arm around her shoulders. She glances up at me. "I thought this might be more comfortable for you."

Haddie rests her head on my shoulder. "Why didn't your mom and dad have more kids?"

"She had complications with me and Dad didn't want to risk losing her, so he said no more after me. I always wanted to grow up with brothers and sisters like Joe did. He'd complain about you guys, and you, especially, were always in his business and he didn't care." I watch the rise and fall of Mom's chest.

"I love my brothers and sister, but being the baby, they've always tried to shield me from everything." She's quiet for a moment. "You know what happened to Abby, don't you?"

That was such a fucked up time for them. I'd never seen Joe cry until the night he showed up on our front steps. We're men, so we don't show our emotions very often, but it was after they got the call that she'd been assaulted. Joe was ready to tear apart the whole town looking for the guy. Instead, my dad took us to a friend's boxing ring and we went round for round until we both collapsed.

"Yeah, I know what happened. It makes sense they'd get protective after that."

It isn't long after that when I feel Haddie's body go slack. I reach over and turn the light down to a soft dim. I lay my head back and close my eyes.

* * *

I BLINK AWAY the sleep and am hot, but it takes me a second to remember what's happening. I'm in my parents' bedroom. I look down and Haddie is sleeping with her head against my chest, and my arms are wrapped around her. I need to piss, but I don't want to wake her.

I look toward the bed and find my mom is awake staring at me. She smiles. "Good morning, baby."

"Good morning. How are you feeling?" I'm always scared of her answer.

She closes her eyes for a minute and then looks at me. "She's something else, isn't she? Such a beautiful young lady."

My fingers itch to stroke her soft looking curls, and I just ball my hand into a fist. "Uh yeah." I clear my throat. "Yes, she's gorgeous."

Gently, I shake her awake. She looks fucking adorable at first because her eyes are clouded with sleep. Haddie's cheek is red from where it rested on my chest. It's like suddenly she remembers what happened because her spine stiffens and her cheeks turn bright pink. She looks to Mom. "I'm sorry, have you been up long?" She gets up and goes to Mom's bedside.

"I just got up. Can you help me into the bathroom?" We both help her stand. They disappear into the bathroom and I head to the kitchen to start a pot of coffee.

It's done brewing when Haddie steps into the kitchen. "I'm so sorry I fell asleep."

I pour her a cup. "That's okay. You're allowed to sleep." The front door opens and Dad comes walking in. He looks exhausted. "Dad? I thought you weren't going to be home until later this morning."

Haddie hands him her coffee. "Thank you, sweetheart." He looks at me. "I couldn't wait so I rented a car and drove home first thing."

The three of us head toward the bedroom. Mom is propped up on some pillows. Haddie and I step into the room first. "Mom, I've got a surprise for you."

Dad comes walking in. "Hi, baby."

Mom's face lights up and she holds her hands out. "Robert, you're home."

"Hi my love." He sits down next to her hips and pulls her into his arms. They whisper quietly to each other, and when I look at Haddie she smiles softly with her eyes bright with unshed tears. We step out into the hall, shutting the door behind us.

"Your mom looked so happy," she says as we walk back to the kitchen.

Haddie sits down at the breakfast bar, drinking her coffee. Neither of us speaks as we sip the hot bitter brew.

I'm pouring my second cup when my dad comes into the kitchen. He stops next to Haddie. "Thank you for staying and helping Madison."

She smiles up at him. "It was my pleasure. Chris stayed and helped." Haddie turns that smile on me and it does something weird to my chest.

Haddie excuses herself and disappears into the family room, returning moments later with her backpack over her shoulder. "I'm going, if that's okay."

"Yes, of course. Thank you again." Dad pulls an envelope out of his pocket and tried to hand it to her. "This is for you."

"Mr. Anderson, I can't take this." She tries to push it back toward him. I don't think she knows how stubborn my dad can be.

He shakes his head. "Please. It would make us so happy if you treated yourself to something nice, or hell, whatever you want. Please." Dad ends in a whisper.

Haddie nods. "Thank you."

"Come on and I'll walk you out." We stop by my parents' bedroom first for Haddie to say goodbye to my mom.

They share a hug and softly spoken words before she stands up. "I'll see you Monday."

"That sounds good, honey. Give my love to that family of yours, and thank your mom again for the soup she brought over."

We're both silent as we step outside. She throws her backpack in the passenger seat and shuts the door. Haddie surprises me when she wraps her arms around me. "Take care of her." She kisses my cheek and then climbs in her car and drives away.

HADDIE

I stare down at my notes and they might as well have been written in different language. This past week I've been tested both emotionally and mentally. Madison Anderson is actively dying and it freaking sucks. I shouldn't have been the one to see her due to our families being friends, but I thought they'd be more comfortable with someone familiar.

In such a short time I've become so attached to her, to them. Every time I've been over there, Chris has been there. He and his dad both look so exhausted and I know neither of them are working anymore. It's basically a waiting game.

I was there yesterday and she hadn't been awake for more than five minutes the whole day. They had me just give her a little bit of a sponge bath and then I made Chris and his dad lunch, making sure both of them ate.

I keep waiting for the phone call I know is coming. My stomach is always cramping, constantly one giant knot, and I can only imagine what it's like for Chris and Robert. I give up on studying, grab my Kindle, and head outside onto the front stoop.

Again, I can't seem to focus on anything. My mind is only on the Anderson family. I've seen lots of patients since I became a homecare aide, especially patients that were close to dying, but never one that I knew before.

I was supposed to see her today, but she wasn't doing well and Robert cancelled my visit. I've been debating on texting Chris, he gave me his number earlier this week, but I haven't used it. If things are bad, I don't want to disrupt them.

"Hey Haddie." I turn to find Lance standing in his doorway. He looks at me closely and steps further outside. "You okay?" Lance lights a cigarette and comes around to stand in front of me.

"Yeah, I just have a lot on my mind. I'm supposed to be studying but I couldn't focus."

Lance takes a deep drag from his cigarette and blows it out. "I'm having some friends and their girls over tonight if you want to have a drink with us."

What could it hurt? It would definitely keep my mind off of things. "Yeah, maybe."

He smiles and pumps his fist. "Yes." Lance snuffs out his cigarette. "I hope you do. I think you'd have a good time."

"I promise I'll really think about it."

Lance heads back into his apartment and I head back into mine. I decide to lay down for a little bit because I may go to the party. I crawl onto my full-size bed. Closing my eyes, I take some slow, deep breaths. I continue to do it until I feel myself fade into dreamland.

My phone ringing wakes me from my slumber. I grab it and see my mom's name on the screen. "Hi, Mom," I yawn as I sit up.

"Hi, baby." My stomach turns as I take in the tone of her voice. "Joe just called and Madison passed away this morning."

I cover my mouth to hide the cry that slips from my lips.

"Joe said she didn't suffer and that it was peaceful." I grab my pillow and bury my face in it as I cry for Madison and cry for Robert and Chris. "Baby girl, are you okay?"

Pulling the pillow away from my face, I shake my head. Of course she can't see that. "No," I croak. Mom must pull the phone away from her mouth because I hear her talking, but it's muffled for a moment. "Honey, go pack a bag, your brother is on his way to get you."

I know she's talking about Parker because Joe will obviously be with the Andersons.

"No, I-I'm okay, I just want to be alone right now." She protests but I insist. I can't lean on them forever. Hanging up before my mom can say anything else, I toss my phone to the end of the bed, ignoring it when it begins to ring again.

I'm not sure how long I cry for, but long enough to have a terrible headache. Walking numbly into my bathroom, I grab some ibuprofen, then swallow them down with water from the sink.

In the kitchen, I grab my ice mask out of the freezer. I lie on my back in my bed and let the mask do its thing, or at least until my face feels numb. After tossing it to the side, I pick up my phone and thumb through my contacts until I find Chris's name. I decide not to call, just send him a quick message.

Haddie: Hey Chris it's Haddie Carmichael. I just wanted to tell you that I'm so very sorry about your mom. I enjoyed what time I got to spend with her. If you or your dad needs anything please don't hesitate to call.

Instead of sending it I delete the message. It sounded really stupid. Maybe I should take them something, but what? They're probably not going to do any cooking, so maybe I could make something to take to them.

I quickly make a list before brushing my hair out and braiding it before brushing my teeth. Heading out to my car,

I make the quick trek to the grocery store. I get everything to make baked spaghetti and the basic staples for sandwiches, lunch meat, bread, cheese and condiments. As I wipe everything up, I send my brother, Joe, a quick text knowing that he was over there earlier.

Haddie: Hey big brother. Are you still with Chris and Robert?

It takes a minute before the black dots start bouncing.

Joe: Yeah, we're keeping his dad company. Why?

Haddie: I thought I'd bring them dinner and some stuff for sandwiches so they don't have to worry about cooking.

Joe: That's sweet of you. I'll let them know you're coming.

It takes me an hour before the spaghetti is done. I stick it in a little carrier that Mom bought me to carry my brownies in. I grab the bags with everything else and carry it all out to my car.

"Hey Haddie are you gonna come tonight?" Lance asks from behind me.

I turn to face him. "I'm going to try. My brother's best friend just lost his mom, so I'm taking them dinner. I'll stop by when I get home."

We say goodbye and I head across town to the Anderson home. I park next to Joe's SUV and climb out. I grab all of the bags, and as I approach the front door it opens, and my brother is standing there.

"Here let me take those." He divests me of my bags and I step inside the house. I rub my arms because it feels heavy as soon as I clear the doorway. "They're in the family room." Joe tells me.

I step around the corner and find Chris stretched out on one sofa while his dad sits hunched over in one of the chairs. They both turn as I step inside.

Robert stands up first as I approach. My eyes burn

because the sadness comes off him in waves. "I-I'm so sorry Robert." He pulls me into a bear hug.

"Thank you for taking such good care of her. She enjoyed your visits." He kisses my forehead. "What's that delicious smell?"

With my arm looped through his I lead him to the kitchen island and have him take a seat. "It's my mom's baked spaghetti."

Chris joins us and I go to him, giving him a hug. Neither of us says anything I just try to provide him comfort. When we separate, I make him sit with his dad and Joe. I grab plates and start dishing up food and set it down in front of all of them.

I watch as Chris and his dad both pick at their food, taking the occasional bite. They're both so sad and I wish there was something I could say or do that could help ease their pain, but there's not. They have to just grieve at their own speed.

While the three of them eat or pretend to eat, I unpack the groceries I bought and put them in the refrigerator. "What's all that?" Robert asks from behind me.

"I-I just got you some bread, lunchmeat, cheese, and condiments for sandwiches." I shrug. "You're not going to want to cook, but you need to eat." My face heats up and tears well up in my eyes because a single tear slides down his cheek.

I wrap my arms around him, hugging him tight as he begins to cry. I close my eyes and just let him get it out. A hand touches my shoulder and I find Chris standing there. "Dad?"

Robert turns to his son, who pulls him into a hug. Joe wraps his arm around my shoulders while we watch father and son hold on tight to each other. Chris mouths that he'll be right back. He leads his father out of the room.

"I didn't mean to make him cry," I say quietly.

Joe kisses my forehead and hugs me to his side. "You didn't. He's just very raw right now. The food was delicious, by the way."

I smile up at him. "Thanks. How's Chloe feeling?"

"She's ready to have the baby. I'm ready for him to get here, but I'm scared to death."

It's so weird to see my big strong brother look so insecure. "You're going to be a great father. Look at the role model you have. Your little boy is going to be one lucky kid." I hug him tight.

Chris comes out a few minutes later. His eyes are redrimmed and bloodshot. I don't hesitate to pull away from Joe and go right to Chris, wrapping my arms around him.

He sighs and then rests his cheek on top of my head. We stay like this until my brother clears his throat, causing Chris and I to step back from each other. Joe looks between us with a curious look on his face.

I grab my purse. "I'm going to go. I'll see you Wednesday," I tell them before heading to the door.

Stepping outside, I take a deep breath, proud that I kept it semi together. I'll have a fresh cry when I get home and then head downstairs to have a couple of drinks with Lance and his friends.

Chris stops me as I reach my door handle. "I wanted to thank you again for the food. That was really thoughtful. It'll be nice not to worry about cooking for ourselves." He leans down, kissing my cheek before he disappears back into the house.

The whole drive home I can still feel my cheek tingling from his kiss...weird.

CHRIS

I stare blindly at the casket in front of me as the pastor from my grandparents' church talks about well...I'm not really even listening. The funeral home did a wonderful job and she looked healthy, beautiful, and like she was sleeping.

My dad, understandably so, lost it and openly wept. I worry about him, and how he's going to handle being without her. Hell, what am I going to do without her? I have no clue, but I miss her terribly already. My dreams are plagued with visions of her slipping away from me.

Last night I dreamt that it wasn't my mom slipping away from me, but Haddie Carmichael. She's willowy as it is, and watching her become skeletal caused me to wake up with a start. I wasn't sure why she was on my mind, but she's my best friend's baby sister, and she needed to get out before I got myself into trouble.

At the end of the service, the pallbearers, Joe, his brother Parker, their dad, and a couple of my cousins get Mom's casket on the cart or whatever it is called. My dad and I follow behind them right out of the church.

We climb into the limousine along with my mom's brother, Charles. My maternal grandparents died when I was still a kid. My dad's dad is the only one left of his side, and he climbs in, sitting beside his brother-in-law.

I watch the passing scenery as we make our way toward the cemetery. I don't know how my dad's going to survive this. I practically had to get him dressed today. He's not sleeping, but granted it's only been four days since she passed.

When we reach the burial site we all get out and slowly make our way to the black awning and take our seats in the front row. My stomach pitches as I stare at the hole that's right in front of me.

The graveside service goes quickly and I keep it together until my dad goes up to the casket with a red rose. He bends down and kisses the wood. "I'll love you forever, my beautiful Madison." Dad steps back slowly and I can tell it's killing him to do so.

I get up and walk right past Dad, kissing the coffin as well. "I love you, Mom. Thank you for giving me so much love."

I look at all of the people who came, and the one person who comes into focus is Haddie, who is standing with her sister, Abby. Her eyes are red, like she's been crying or is about to. There's an invisible pull that's telling me to go to her, to comfort her, but I see Joe watching me, watching her.

I give him a chin lift and walk toward my dad, then lead him off to the side. We watch everyone stop and touch my mom's coffin, saying their own goodbyes. My uncle leads my dad to the limo and I stand right where I'm at and watch them lower her into the ground.

My heart beats a mad, angry rhythm in my chest and all I want to do is tilt my head back and scream bloody murder. I close my eyes and will the feeling to go away, but it doesn't—not until a soft, slender hand grabs hold of mine.

"It doesn't seem like it now, but things will get better." Her voice is soft and melodic, soothing the anger that wants to escape.

I squeeze her hand before letting go. I'm not sure why there's all of a sudden this—this, I don't know what it is, but there's something there between us—it's just not a good time, and she's too young for me.

With a hand on the small of her back I lead her to her family. Haddie and Joe's mom hugs me tight. "If you need anything, anything at all, don't hesitate to call us or come over."

"Thanks, JoJo." I shake Dylan's and Ben's hands before kissing Abby on the cheek. Joe pulls me into a back slapping hug. "Thanks for being there for me, brother. I love ya, man," I say quietly.

"I've always got your back, okay?" He slaps me on the back and then I head to the limo.

* * *

I HOLD the straw to my nose and inhale the white powder up each nostril before rubbing some that was left on the mirror on my gums. I grab my tumbler filled with bourbon and swallow it down.

My phone rings, and when I pick it up, I see it's Joe. I'm not in any condition to talk to him—I'm too fucking high and he's a cop. I know he'd never arrest me, but I don't want to put him in an awkward position.

Plus he's living in his happy bubble since his son was born a few weeks ago. I, unfortunately, haven't met the little guy because I've been too much of a mess.

It's been a month since we buried my mom and I'm in a

freefall. I know it and I just can't muster up the energy to care or stop the fall. Luckily my job has been understanding, but I don't think that'll last too much longer if I don't get my shit together.

My dad's surprisingly doing okay, or as okay as a man can be after losing the love of his life. I pour myself another glass and drink it down. Tonight, I should've gone out, found some pussy, and buried my troubles between their thighs, but I'd be terrible company.

Leaning my head on the back of the sofa, I wait for the alcohol to work its magic.

* * *

I OPEN my eyes to the sound of my front door closing. "What the fuck?" I groan. Pushing up, I sit on the side of the bed. When did I come to bed? I stand up and realize I'm naked and my bedroom reeks of sex.

Stumbling into my bathroom, I take a piss before climbing into the shower. I stand under the stream of hot water, letting it relax my sore, stiff muscles. Who was here? I'm freaked out that I have no clue what happened last night.

After my shower I feel semi-human and throw on cut off sweatpants and a sleeveless t-shirt. In the living room I don't see my blow out—I hope it's because I hid it.

Fuck, what happened? I can't remember shit. I think I need to "Just say no" for a bit. I'm a dumbfuck who had sex last night and can't remember it.

I pick up the rest of the garbage and am taking out the trash when the front door opens. "Oh great, you're up. I figured you might be hungry."

Turning my head I watch Haddie Carmichael walk toward me carrying a bag and a drink carrier. She sets everything down on the table and turns to face me. I scan her over closely and see that she looks sexy.

Her strawberry blonde curls are wild, hanging over her shoulders. Haddie's lips look swollen, like she's been thoroughly kissed and fucked, but there is no way it was me who did it...right?

"Aren't you going to eat?" She shifts nervously as she stares at me.

I take a deep breath. "Haddie, what happened last night? Why are you here?"

Her face pales and I immediately feel like shit. "You-You don't remember?" she whispers.

There is no way I could lie to her. "I was really fucked up," I say as I shake my head. "Did we fuck?"

"I-I sh-should probably get going. Enjoy the food." She's out the front door before I can stop her.

I should go after her, make sure she's okay, but this is for the best. I'm a mess right now and Haddie doesn't need that. I hope the sex was at least good for her. On that thought I grab the containers she left and dig into the pancakes. Fuck, these are exactly what I needed, and I completely ignore how shitty I feel.

Once I finish breakfast, I slam some coffee before taking the other container of food over to my dad's—my dad's, not my parents', just my dad. My eyes burn, but I quickly blink it away.

I pull a mint out of the glovebox and pop it into my mouth as I drive toward Dad's.

Pulling into the driveway I see the grass is overgrown. I'll mow it while I'm here. I grab my keys and let myself in. "Dad?" I holler.

"Chris?" I turn to find my dad coming down the hall. "This is a nice surprise. What're you doing here?"

I hold up the container. "I had some leftover pancakes

and thought I'd share." He smiles as he takes them from me. I follow behind him into the kitchen, that's a mess. "What's going on here? Do you need me to hire you a housekeeper?"

Dad shrugs. "I don't know. I guess. I've gone back to work and I'm trying to play catch up, which means I'm not here a lot."

"I'll make some calls," I tell him as I pour myself a cup of coffee. I hold the pot up to him. "Do you need a warmup?"

"Yes, please." I top him off before taking the seat next to him, watching as he digs into the pancakes. "You look tired, son."

"Gee, thanks, Dad."

Dad shakes his head. "I wasn't trying to be mean…I swear. You just look wore out."

I don't know what to say because the last thing he needs is to worry about me when he's still grieving the loss of his wife. I need to be strong in case he's not. "I promise I'm good. I had a few drinks and stayed up too late and got up too early. That's all, I promise. "

While Dad cleans up the kitchen after he finishes eating, I head outside and mow the grass. It takes me a long time to get the whole yard done, but it looks a lot better when I'm finished.

I put the mower away and make my way back inside. My dad hands me a bottle of water and I hope he can't tell that my hands are trembling slightly. Fuck, I haven't ever been blackout drunk. I fucked someone, a someone I shouldn't have, and I don't fucking remember any of it.

The last thing I do remember is doing that last rail and leaning back on my sofa.

"Son? Are you okay?" I shake myself out of my thoughts to find my dad staring at me, concern written all over his face.

"I'm okay—just hot and tired. Do you want to order some takeout?"

He smiles. "That sounds good. You know what I like."

We end up ordering Thai from a little restaurant downtown and I spend the night with Dad, watching movies, and smoking cigars. What I don't do is think about Haddie and trying to remember what happened between us. It freaks me out, having that blank spot in my mind.

HADDIE

I step inside my apartment, drop my purse on the floor, and after locking my door, I collapse onto my sofa. "You're such an idiot," I mutter. I grab one of my pillows, hold it over my head, and scream into it.

I'm not impulsive—ever. Why did I have to become impulsive now, and with my brother's best friend no less, someone who doesn't even remember taking my virginity last night? Of course, I basically threw it at him.

When Chris texted me last night I was surprised. I hadn't seen him since the funeral.

Chris: Hey, what are you up to?

I stare down at my phone, shocked that Chris just texted me. He's been a ghost since Madison passed. Of course, I don't blame him. I've stopped by to see Robert the past couple of weeks and he seems to be doing okay.

I've always brought something to eat—just wanting to make sure Robert is eating properly. He seems to enjoy the company and I'm glad. I won't lie that when I've been there I've hoped that Chris would show up, but he hasn't.

Haddie: Nothing, stranger. How are you?

The dots begin dancing and then his next message pops up.

Chris: Hanging in there. Do you want to come over and hang out?

Wow, I wasn't expecting that, but I'm kind of glad he asked. I've been thinking about him a lot lately.

Haddie: Sure, do you want me to bring anything?

Chris: I only have booze and water, so if you want something different you might want to grab it.

Chris texts me his address and I run into the bathroom, quickly brushing my teeth, and then shaking out my hair before pulling it back into a low ponytail. I'm in black short knit shorts and a fitted gray t-shirt that says "My brother is a cop. What does yours do?" in red.

Mom had them made for us when Joe graduated from the academy. I slip my feet into a pair of flip flops, grab my purse, and a Coke Zero before heading out. By the time I make it to Chris's the butterflies in my belly have taken flight.

Why am I nervous? I've known him all my life.

When I pull into his driveway a short time later I grab my drink and climb out of my car. The front door opens as I approach. I don't want to admit that he looks really hot in his jogging shorts and sleeveless t-shirt. His blond hair is messy and I don't miss the stubble on his face.

Chris grabs my hand when I reach the steps and he quickly pulls me inside. He wraps his arms around me, hugging me tight. "Thanks for coming over."

I don't miss the smell of booze on him, but it is Saturday and he's entitled to cocktails after a busy work week, I'm sure. He finally lets me go and I look around his living room. I'm surprised to see it's kind of a mess.

"Come sit with me." He leads me over to the sofa and I sit

on one side and he sits on the other. "Dad says you've been visiting him. He really enjoys that."

I smile. "I'm glad. He's a great man." Turning to face him I ask, "How are you really doing?"

He looks away from me, but then turns back. "I miss her. Sometimes I dream about her and I swear I can smell her perfume when I wake up." His voice cracks and I make the decision to scooch closer, putting my hand on top of his.

"Have you thought about grief counseling? Sometimes talking to strangers going through what you went through could be helpful."

Chris shakes his head. "No, I don't think I want to do that. Do you want to watch a movie?"

I notice he's really jittery. Is he nervous too? No, that can't be possible. I've heard the stories about him and how much he likes women. He leans back and I do the same as he looks through the movies.

We decide on Jurassic World, with Chris Pratt, yummy. As the sky darkens outside, the inside of the house does too. I turn my head to look at Chris and find his head tipped back, staring at the ceiling.

Scooting even closer, I grab his hand. "Are you okay?"

Chris shakes his head and then I watch one tear slide down his cheek. I grab him and pull him into a hug. His whole body trembles as he buries his face in my neck. He's not crying, but he's battling some sort of emotional war inside.

My hand slides up into his hair and I stroke his head, surprised how soft his hair is beneath my fingers. We say nothing and I just let him work out whatever is going on in his head.

I continue stroking his hair and freeze when I feel his lips on my neck. Goosebumps pop up all over my skin. Chris kisses up my neck until he reaches my ear. "You're so beautiful, Haddie."

Pulling back enough to look into his eyes I make a quick, impulsive decision—I grab Chris's face and pull him to me, kissing him on his lips. He immediately takes control of the kiss.

Sure, I've been kissed before, but it's been only a couple of times and they were boys, not men like Chris. He forces my mouth open with his and his tongue swoops in, causing me to moan.

A small voice inside is telling me to stop this, but there's this tiny voice telling me that I should take whatever he's offering because who knows if I'll ever get another chance—oh, I know I will eventually, but this, this could be my chance to get my first time out of the way. Plus it's with someone I've known all my life—someone who would hopefully handle me with care.

Chris pulls me until I'm straddling his lap, coming in contact with his hard dick. He moans into my mouth and I feel it vibrate all the way down into my nether regions. His hands move down my back to my non-existent ass. He manages to find some ass to grab onto and rocks me on his dick.

He hits my clit and I mew against his mouth. His hands slide up my backside and then dip into my shorts, grabbing my bare ass. A full body shiver wracks my body and I feel wetness between my legs.

"Wrap your legs around me," Chris whispers with his lips against mine.

I do as he says and suddenly he's up and carrying me through his house. He lowers himself with me still attached to him until my back hits his mattress.

My heart pounds wildly in my chest. It's dusk, so I'm able to see him barely as he stares down at me. The look on his face is intense. I don't know what to do, so I reach up and cup his cheek. "You are so handsome."

What is happening? This is Chris the douche, but right now there's this…this thing between us.

He leans further into my hand and then turns his head to kiss the palm. "You feel it, don't you?" Chris asks and all I can do is nod.

This time when we begin to kiss he's lying on top of me with my long legs wrapped around him. I should stop him and tell him I'm a virgin, but he grinds against me and my mind goes blank.

My hands roam down his back and then up under his t-shirt. His skin is warm under my fingers. With one hand, Chris reaches between us and inside my shorts, then panties. He swirls his fingers through the wet and then rubs circles around my clit.

With a surprised cry I come and come hard, riding his finger as he pushes it inside of me. "Fuck, you're tight." I continue riding his finger until my orgasm begins to fade.

When he pulls his finger from my shorts, he sucks the digit into his mouth. He moans as he licks it clean and I swear I have a baby orgasm. Once he's done, he quickly pulls off his t-shirt and then pulls me up to pull off mine and then he unhooks my bra.

I move to cover my breasts but he stops me. "Fuck, you're pretty. I have to be inside you."

My heart pounds as he pulls off my shorts and panties. Am I ready to do this? The first time is supposed to be awful, should I just get it over with? He pushes up onto his knees and then slides off of the bed. I watch as he pulls his shorts down.

His penis looks huge. I'm not sure it'll fit, but I at least want to try. Chris climbs back up on the bed, dips his head and licks my pussy. I cry out because I've never felt something so incredible. In no time I come again, incredibly fast. I should feel embarrassed, but I feel boneless right now, and can't pull up the energy to care.

Chris kisses up my body and stops, sucking first one nipple into his mouth, swirling his tongue around the tip. Then he moves to the other, giving it the same treatment. I arch my back, pushing it deeper into his mouth.

All too soon he travels back up until he reaches my mouth. Our kiss is heated, intense, and then I feel him at my pussy. I know it's painful at first, and lucky for me my body is languid—when he eases inside of me I squeeze my eyes shut. It burns and feels like I'm being split in two.

He pulls almost all of the way out before slamming into me to the hilt. I cry out against his mouth. "Did I hurt you?" Chris whispers against my lips.

Honestly, it didn't hurt as bad as I thought it would, I just feel stuffed full. I shake my head, "No, please move," I plead.

Chris begins to move, hitting my clit with every thrust. I grab onto his biceps as he begins to pick up the pace. The bed rocks and the headboard knocks against the wall with each thrust.

I've never felt something so good. He again reaches between us and begins rubbing my clit. How is it possible that I feel like I could come again? He rolls us with himself still buried inside of me until I'm straddling him and have no clue what I'm supposed to do.

He grabs my hips and starts guiding me, and shit, it feels like he's deeper inside of me. My head flies back and I groan as he lets go of me with one hand and reaches his arms around me.

Chris rolls us again as I begin to come and then begins to fuck me at a punishing pace. When he comes he plants himself to the root and I feel him jerk inside of me.

He pulls out of me and then pulls me into his arms and

kisses my forehead. "Thank you for coming over tonight," Chris says in the quiet of the room.

"Of course." I lean up and kiss his lips.

Chris hugs me tight and promptly falls asleep.

I shake my head, no longer wanting to think about that night. I get up off the sofa and go into my bedroom and climb into bed, maybe, just maybe I'll forget the colossal mistake I made last night.

HADDIE

I yawn loudly as I try to pay attention during my Pharmacology class. My teacher looks pointedly at me before moving on to the next topic. While she talks it seriously sounds like the adults on Charlie Brown talking. I don't know what my problem is, but I'm so exhausted.

Second semester just started four weeks ago and it's been six weeks since I've heard from Chris. I've tried calling him and texting him, but he's obviously ignoring me. What did I expect, giving my virginity to someone who has always been a grade A douche?

That night he was so sweet and he needed me. I thought we'd had a connection—he even said he felt it, but I guess he was only feeling the desire to have sex, nothing more.

At least my first time is over and done with and it was at least good—no, it was great. I've heard too many horror stories about how horrible a girl's first time can be. Shit, my sister's first time was her sexual assault.

I try to focus back in on my professor but honestly, I couldn't tell you what she's even talked about. When she dismisses us, I shove everything into my backpack and head out into the hall.

When I make my way outside I find Graham sitting on a bench. "Hey you." He smiles when I approach and my stomach does little flips, and not the good kind.

"Hi pretty lady. How was class?" Graham and I have struck up a nice friendship. I honestly don't want anything more and it feels weird to think about dating someone because I never really have before. The closest I've ever been to a relationship and you can't even call it that was what went down with you know who.

I yawn. "It was fine, but I'm in desperate need of a nap."

"We can skip lunch," he says while we walk to the parking lot toward our vehicles.

"No, I'm starving. It'll just need to be a quick lunch, if that's okay?" We stop next to mine.

I follow Graham to Subway and gorge myself on a six-inch turkey on wheat with everything. "Wow, you were really hungry," he says as I crumple up my wrapper and shove it inside my empty chip bag.

"Sorry," I say, ducking my head because I'm embarrassed I just inhaled all of that in front of him.

He grabs my wrist. "Don't be sorry and don't be embarrassed. You're hungry, eat." By the time he finishes I can't stop yawning. Graham walks me out to my car. "Are you sure you're okay driving home?"

"I'll seriously be fine. My apartment isn't that far from here. I'll see you Monday." I climb into my car and give him a wave before pulling out of the parking lot.

Once I'm home, I grab my bag, sling it over my shoulder, and head up the stairs to my apartment. Inside, I drop my bag on the sofa and go directly to my bed. I'm out the moment I hit my pillow.

* * *

TEARS BLUR my vision as I stare at the positive pregnancy test in my hand. How could I let this happen? My parents are going to be so disappointed in me. Oh god, I'm pregnant with Chris's baby. I gave him my virginity and he didn't even remember doing it.

I pick up my phone and quickly dial my sister. "Hey Haddie, what's up?"

"C-Can I come o-over? I'm in trouble, Abby." I don't know what else to say right now.

"What's going on? Do I need to call Ben or Joe?"

I shake my head even though she can't see it. "No, nothing like that."

"Okay, just get here, okay?" Her voice is soft, but firm.

We hang up and I put together a bag to take over to her house. In the bathroom, I dry my face and take a deep breath. After I squirt some Visine into my eyes, I grab my stuff and head over to Abby's, she'll know what to do.

By the time I pull into my sister's driveway the tears are flowing again. I have four and a half months left of school and now I'm going to finish the hardest part pregnant.

The front door opens as I climb out of the car. Abby's brow is furrowed as she takes me in. She pulls me into a hug as soon as I step through the door. I bury my face in my sister's neck as the tears flow. "Come sit down, sweetheart."

"W-Where are the kids?"

"After you called I asked Ben's mom to come get them for a little bit." She takes a seat next to me and grabs my hand. "Tell me what's going on."

I take a deep breath. "I'm pregnant."

Abby's mouth opens and closes. "Are you sure?"

I nod. "The test says I am and my period is two weeks late." Tears spill down my cheeks. "What am I gonna do?"

Abby brushes some of my hair back behind my ear. "Who's the father?"

I don't want to tell her, but if I'm going to tell anyone it would be her, my best friend, my sister. "It's bad. Abby, it's Chris."

She looks at me and tilts her head to the side. "Chris?" It dawns on her because her eyes widen comically, too bad I don't find any of this funny. "Oh god, Chris Anderson? Joe's best friend?"

I nod and begin to cry again. Abby pulls me into a tight hug and strokes a hand over my hair. The tears stop a few minutes later and I pull away from her and look down at my lap.

"Honey, how did this happen? You were a virgin not too long ago."

"It was about a month after Madison passed away. He texted me out of the blue and asked if I wanted to come over. He was just so sad. I was hugging him and the next thing I knew we were kissing and then things just kind of spiraled from there."

Abby scooches closer to me. "Did you tell him no, or tell him to stop?" I hate that this even made her mind go there.

"I-I encouraged him to keep going. There is something, though." Fuck, I don't want to tell her this part. "Um…I didn't realize he was drunk and he doesn't, or didn't, remember any of it." Annndd…I'm crying again.

She brushes my hair out of my face. "What do you want to do? I'll support whatever decision you make."

"I want this baby," I whisper, which surprises me—kids were never part of my plans. I figured I'd always just be the fun aunt and that's it. "What am I gonna tell Mom and Dad? They're going to hate me."

Abby pulls my hands up to her mouth and kisses them. "I'll go with you to tell them and they're not going to hate you. I can't guarantee that Joe won't lose his mind, but he's living in his newborn baby happy bubble, so you may not have to worry about him—no matter what we all love you."

"Can we go over to Mom and Dad's now? I want to get it over with," I tell her.

She nods, and then stands up. "Let's do it."

* * *

TEARS RUN down my cheeks as the sound of the front door slamming echoes through the house. I just told my parents about the baby and my mom started to cry and hugged me. Dad looked at me and several looks passed over his face—none that I could decipher—and then he stormed out.

I sob as my mom and sister try to comfort me. "Please take me back to my car," I tell Abby. I hate people seeing me like this.

"Okay, honey." She wraps her arm around my waist.

Mom follows us out to the car and opens the passenger side door for me. "I'll talk to Daddy, okay?" she says before pulling me into a hug. "It's going to be okay. Babies are a blessing. We're here for you. Can you tell me who the father is?" Mom asks softly.

I shake my head. "I want to tell him first."

"Okay, honey. Abby, make sure she's okay to drive before you let her leave," she says, looking across the roof at my sister.

"Of course. Love you, Mom."

Once we're on the road I rest my head against the window, closing my eyes. Abby grabs my hand. "It's going to be okay. I promise I won't tell anyone that Chris is the father. Do you want me to go with you when you tell him?"

"No, I should probably tell him by myself."

"I'm here if you need anything," she says as she pulls into

her driveway. I climb out and my body feels heavy. I feel exhausted. At least that all makes sense now and I know there is an end in sight.

I loved doing my OB rotation and even got to help deliver a baby, but I never really wanted or thought about having one of my own. When I climb out of Abby's car, I shut the door and walk around to mine.

"Call me," Abby tells me.

Instead of driving home I decide to go over to Chris's to tell him about the baby—it's best to just do it quick, like ripping a band-aid off. It sucks that he doesn't remember any part of that night. I pull up his address and then plug it into my GPS, just in case I can't remember how to get there.

When I reach his house butterflies take flight in my belly. I'm really not sure how he's going to react, but I need to just get it over with. I climb out of my car and head up to the front door.

I ring the doorbell and then wait for him to answer. After a couple of minutes I knock on the door and again no answer, but the door must not have been shut all of the way, because knocking on it pushed it open a bit. I push it open and call out, "Chris?"

The place is a mess—empty bottles of all types litter the coffee table. A mirror with white powder on it sits amongst the bottles. I place a hand on my queasy stomach and move through the living room.

"Chris, are you here?"

I reach his bedroom and push open the door to find him sitting on the edge of his bed, completely nude. I don't miss the naked feminine bodies lying face down in his bed. My eyes burn. Even though I have no right to be upset, I'm crushed.

"What are you doing here?" His voice is rough from sleep. Chris stands up and I bite my lip to keep from gasping. He looks terrible; his skin has lost its natural glow—it's pale, sallow. He's got the beginnings of a gut where his six pack used to be. His eyes are so bloodshot they look red.

"I-I need to talk to you." God, do I even want to tell him about the baby? Yes, he needs to know, and know I'm not afraid to do it alone.

I look away as he grabs some shorts off the floor and throws them on. "Sure, let me make some coffee."

He walks by me and I follow him into the kitchen. I wrap my arms around myself, and take a deep breath. "This isn't easy, so I just need to say it. Um…I'm—I'm pregnant, and it's yours." Chris freezes. "I don't expect anything from you. You're clearly in no position to be someone's dad."

Chris stands frozen in his spot and doesn't react at all.

"Did you hear me? I'm pregnant, it's your baby." I wait a few minutes for him to speak, but he doesn't say anything. I move toward him, stopping a few feet away. "What's happened to you?"

I don't bother waiting for his non-answer and turn around, walking out. "Looks like it's going to be just me and you," I whisper.

I can do this…I think.

CHRIS

"*S*on, I'm worried about you." I look up at my dad from my place on the sofa. "You look like shit and I'm worried you're slowly killing yourself. This is not what your mother would want."

He's right, I know he is, but I can't seem to stop myself. I'm spiraling out of control. It's been two weeks since Haddie showed up and rocked my world. She's pregnant with my baby. A night I was so fucked up I don't even remember, I slept with her, and planted my baby in her belly.

Instead of getting my shit together I went on a major bender that ended with me waking up in a pool of my own vomit.

"You need to go to treatment before you die on me, leaving me all alone." Dad's voice cracks, and I hate that I'm the cause of the pain in his voice.

The front door flies open, causing us both to jump. Joe comes storming in, followed by his dad. "You knocked up my fucking sister." He strikes fast, punching me in the face twice. "How could you fucking touch her?" He gets one more punch in before his dad is there.

Mr. Carmichael pulls him off me and my dad moves to stand in front of me. "Son, is this true?"

"I do-don't remember it. I was fucked up, and I guess I texted her and she came over. In the morning I woke up and she came back with breakfast." I look at Joe and his dad. "I swear to god I wouldn't have touched her. I'm so fucking sorry, brother."

"Don't call me that," he growls, but his dad stayed him with a hand on his chest. "We're fucking done, do you hear me? I've protected you, made excuses, but no more. Stay away from me, my family, especially my sister and her baby." Joe looks at my dad. "I'm sorry, Robert." Dylan pulls him out of the house, the door slamming behind them.

My dad gets down on the floor next to me. "Fuck, Dad, I'm so sorry." I begin sobbing. "I'm such a fucking mess. I ruin everything," I whisper the last part.

He pulls me into his arms. "Son, you're sick. You need help, and if you'll let me, I'll get you the help you need."

I nod. "I need help, Dad," I cry loudly, knowing that my mom would be so disappointed in the way I've dealt with her death, or hell, life in general.

"Son, go take a shower. I'm going to make some calls, and we'll see how soon we can get you into a treatment facility."

I nod. "Please don't give up on me." My voice breaks.

He grabs my face. "I won't, son. Now go."

I head into my bedroom, strip out of my clothes, and head to the shower.

* * *

I CLIMB out of the Uber and grab my suitcase out of the trunk. A man with a clipboard comes out, smiling widely as I approach him. "Chris Anderson?" I nod and take his hand. "Welcome to Sunrise Rehabilitation and Wellness. I'm

Damian, and I'll be handling your intake and showing you around the facility."

This morning had been rough when Dad brought me to the airport. He'd wanted to come inside with me, but I needed to do this on my own. I had to be strong enough to get on the plane and head to California to seek treatment.

It was two and half days ago when my best friend in the whole world punched me three times and then walked out of my life. I can't blame him. I'm not the same guy I was before everything got way out of hand. I'm the guy who fucked his baby sister and got her pregnant.

Dad wouldn't leave me after they left. I think he was afraid I was going to kill myself, and to be honest that thought had crossed my mind. I was convinced it was better for everyone. Of course, that was when I realized if I did it, I would leave my dad all alone and I couldn't do that.

At the drop off, Dad pulled me into a bear hug. "I'm so proud of you. You get better and when they let me, I'll be on the first plane out there."

"I won't let you down, Dad," I told him and I meant it.

He gave me another hug before letting me go.

Now I follow Damian inside the rehab center in Calabasas, California. It's beautiful and right on the beach. Of course, I won't see it for a while. I need to go through detox first. Then I'll begin the program and will have a little more freedom.

After the tour they take me over to the detox unit. Damian has me hand my suitcase to a guy who looks to be around my dad's age. "I need to search it," he says before disappearing behind a door.

"I have cigarettes in there. Is that a problem?" I ask Damian as he leads me into an exam room.

"You can't smoke while you're in detox, but there's an area outside that we allow it. Have a seat on the table. We're just going to give you a quick exam, draw some labs, and come up with a treatment plan."

He weighs me and I see that I've put twenty-five pounds on since my mom died. I knew I was looking pretty doughy. Damian has me sit on the exam table and takes my vitals.

"Your blood pressure is a little elevated. When was the last time you used?"

"Uhh…two and a half days ago."

He writes it down. "How much have you been using?"

I scratch my head. "The past couple of weeks I was up to almost two grams of coke every day or every other day. I drink anywhere from an eighteen pack of beer or a bottle of Grey Goose a day." Saying it out loud makes my stomach hurt.

"How often do you blackout?"

I think about Haddie. Haddie who is pregnant with my baby and I don't remember having sex with her at all. Shame fills me and my eyes begin to burn. "Too many times to count."

The staff doctor comes in after I finish answering questions. She looks like someone's grandmother. It's super embarrassing when they do a STD screening because there is nothing better than having a giant Q-tip shoved in the end of your dick, but damn, if I gave Haddie an STD I'd never forgive myself.

Damian takes me to the little kitchen area and grabs me a sandwich, then leads me back to the medical wing. "Have a seat and we'll show you to your room shortly."

I take one bite of the sandwich and throw it in the trash. My appetite is non-existent. As I wait for them to come get me, my knee bounces nervously. I hope this works, I want it to work. My dad doesn't deserve a junkie son. He's already lost the love of his life. I don't think he'd survive losing me too.

* * *

"I'm Chris, and I'm an alcoholic and an addict. I've been sober for fourteen days," I say, looking around the circle of others like me.

They all respond, "Hi Chris."

"My dad sounded so sad when I talked to him this morning. I hate that I'm not there helping him grieve my mother, but I knew if I didn't get help, then I could possibly leave him too." I run a hand over my hair. "I feel clear-headed for the first time since I arrived two weeks ago. I'm determined now more than ever to do the work, follow the steps, and stay sober for me." There is so much work I need to do on myself. I didn't start using because of some trauma, or because my parents used, but because I just liked the way I felt.

I take my seat and listen to Nathan, whose room is next to mine. He was a child actor who was abused by his parents and used to self-medicate. The poor guy OD'd, but luckily his fifteen-year-old son found him and called 9-1-1.

After we finish, I grab my coffee and step out to our smoking area. I light up, and as I blow out the smoke, I stare out at the ocean. Nathan comes to stand next to me, lighting his own cigarette.

Neither of us speaks, we just take in the peace and tranquility of the vast body of water in front of us, it's so beautiful. The breeze feels so good on my face and I feel lighter than I have in a long time.

I snub out my smoke and get ready to head inside when he stops me. "What are your plans when you're done with treatment?"

I turn to look at him. "I don't know. Shit's not really great back home right now." I tell him about Mom, Haddie, Joe, and the baby.

"Fuck. That's intense, man."

I shake my head and swallow down the lump in my throat. "When I finish I don't think I should go back home, not yet at least. I'd be no good to that baby and no good to Haddie. I know I need to make amends, but I need to make sure I'm truly clean and sober. I have to get my shit together and figure out what I want." Nathan sits down on the bench and I sit on the other side.

"My best friend, the guy who helped get in me here, has a construction company. If you want to make California your home for a bit, I bet I could get you a job." He picks at his thumbnail.

"I appreciate the offer, let me think about it." If I stay I'll be leaving my dad alone, but maybe I need to figure out my life. As far as Haddie and the baby goes…I'm no good for her, or the child.

They're better off without me.

HADDIE

One Year Later

"Just call the office if you need anything. The number is on the magnet," I tell the wife of my new patient as I stick my laptop into my bag and head out to my car.

That was my last patient for the day, so I head across town to my parents' house. I pull into the driveway and climb out. I'm exhausted, but it'll be a long time before I'll be able to go to sleep.

I reach the front door and my dad opens it with my baby girl in his arms, snoozing away. "Hey," I whisper. "How was she today?" I stroke a hand over my baby girl's blonde fuzz.

"She was perfect. When I got home, we took a nap and then she ate four ounces. We did some tummy time and then changed her diaper before she passed out again." My dad is one of the world's best grandpas. All his grandbabies love him to pieces, even my little Madison Anne—named after her late grandmother, her father's mom.

Dad reluctantly hands over my four-month-old daughter and I hug her to my chest. She snuggles against me and I kiss the top of her head before inhaling her sweet lavender and chamomile scent.

"Are you going to Robert's next?" Dad asks as he picks the carrier up, placing it on the sofa.

I place Madison in it and smile at my dad. "Yeah, I'm making spaghetti." The baby and I go every night to Chris's dad's home, to visit and then cook him dinner. It works out perfect because after we eat, he gets snuggle time with his granddaughter and I can get my charting done from my visits earlier in the day.

"Tell him not to forget we're going fishing Saturday." Dad and Joe have included Robert in a lot of stuff they do, for which I'm grateful. I know it's been hard on him, having Chris across the country living in California.

We haven't talked since I told him I was pregnant—we've written each other, but they're very formal and weird. He knows we have a daughter and she's named after his mom. Robert's facetimed with him while he's watched Madison, so I know Chris has seen her.

Other than that, he just tells me about his job—he's working for a friend of a friend he met in rehab. Chris was never the type to work with his hands, so the fact that he's working for a construction company, building McMansions, is bizarre, but I'm happy for him.

Robert's tried to show me pictures of Chris in California, but I never look. I'm not sure why, maybe because I mean nothing to him, my daughter means nothing to him. If I see him, I'm not sure how I'd react.

I'm fine raising her alone, I'm just sad that instead of

coming back here after treatment he stayed out there, leaving his father alone.

That's also why my daughter's last name is Carmichael and not Anderson. I cried to Robert when I made that decision, but he was so damn sweet about it and said she was his granddaughter no matter what her last name was.

I'm pulling into the driveway when the front door flies open. Robert comes out, smiling wide. "There's my girls."

"Hi, Robert." I climb out and step right into his arms. He kisses the top of my head. "How was your day?" He's pretty much practicing part-time now. He keeps Madison two days a week and then my mom and/or dad keep her the other two.

I only work four days a week, but it's ten-hour days, which is nice because then I have three days with just my girl.

Motherhood has been a rollercoaster ride, but I've loved every minute. My little girl came into the world surrounded by all three of her grandparents and my big sister.

I had a little post-partum when she was about a month old. I was crying all the time, I wasn't taking care of myself, and I couldn't sleep. Everyone was worried and I hated that I caused that. Mom finally convinced me to get help. Since I'm breastfeeding, I'm on an extremely low dose of an anti-depressants and I began exercising.

I don't feel one hundred percent, but I do feel better than I did.

"It was good, but it's better now." He rushes to the back door. "There's my little girl." Robert's sweet voice makes me smile. Like a seasoned pro he opens the back door, unhooks the carrier, and he carries it toward the house, before I'm even shutting my door. Once inside, Robert stops me in the foyer. "Chris is home—I'm sorry, sweetheart—I had no idea. He wanted to surprise me."

I swallow the lump in my throat and ignore the way my heart begins to race. "It's fine. No worries, okay."

We walk through the house and once we step into the family room I freeze. Chris is standing in the middle of the room, looking better than I've ever seen.

He looks happy, maybe a little nervous, but a lot better than the last time I saw him. I slowly step further into the room. "Um…hey."

"Hi Haddie, you look great." His voice is deep and a little scratchier than I remember. God, I'm a dork—it's only been a year.

Robert joins us with a sleeping Madison in his arms. I lean down, kissing her cheek. I turn to Chris. "This is Madison."

He reaches a shaky hand out, touching her hair lightly. "S-She's more beautiful in person. Can I—can I hold her?"

Robert looks to me and I nod. How could I deny him the chance to hold his daughter? No matter how I feel about him, Chris is still her father. Robert carefully places the baby in his arms.

I watch as he carries her over to the sofa and sits down. He doesn't say anything, just stares down at the beautiful girl we created. Suddenly a deep guttural cry leaves him, and Chris's body begins to shake.

He places his lips against Madison's forehead, tears streaming down his face. Robert wraps his arm around me, hugging me into his side. We watch Chris weep over our sleeping girl.

I don't want to admit that my eyes burn with unshed tears. I tell myself that it's because I wish Madison was here to hold her granddaughter. She's met her, when the baby was a few weeks old, Robert and I took her to the cemetery. We took her picture while she slept in her carrier next to her namesake's tombstone.

The baby starts to fuss, probably feeling her dad's sadness. She waves her little fists in the air before letting loose a high-pitched cry. I want to go to her and take her in my arms, but Chris begins to bounce her in his arms, softly shushing her.

Sure enough, Madison begins to settle. I turn to Robert. "I'm going to start dinner."

He stops me. "Why don't we order out? You always cook for me." I do, but I enjoy it. I want to take care him; I want to do it for Robert's Madison.

"You know I enjoy cooking for you." I kiss his cheek and then head into the kitchen.

As I stir the pasta in the water, Chris joins me. I avoid looking at him as I busy myself at the stove.

"She is so beautiful, Haddie," he says quietly as he leans against the counter. "Is she a good baby?"

I nod. "Yeah, she's pretty perfect." I make a mistake and turn to look at him. Close up he's so beautiful it hurts, and I think our daughter looks just like him.

The natural glow he used to have is back and even more golden than before, but that's what happens when you live in California. His dark blond hair is bleached from the sun and makes him look like a surfer boy. His blue eyes are bright, and his body is bigger—more muscular, but still lean. "H-How long are you home for?"

"I—um—I'm actually home for good. It was time to come home, make things right." He says that last little bit quietly. "I know I have no right to ask, but can I spend time with Madison?"

"Of course. Your dad watches her two days a week and I'm usually here with her in the evenings."

He nods. "Okay, thank you so much." Chris pulls an envelope out of his back pocket and hands it to me. "Dad helped me figure out child support. The check is for back child support, and you'll start receiving money in two to three weeks."

"Um…okay. You didn't have to do this, we're getting by just fine." Don't get me wrong, I'm not too proud to take it and use it toward taking care of our daughter. "But thank you."

I take the envelope over to my backpack, stuffing it inside. Back at the stove, I stare into the pot of noodles, and I can feel him close.

"You look really good," Chris says from behind me. "Motherhood looks good on you."

"T-Thank you. She's given me some much needed curves." I shoot him a hesitant smile. "Um…how's your sobriety going?" I look back down at the stove. "Ugh, I'm sorry, that was a stupid question."

I feel the heat of him as he steps closer. "It wasn't stupid. It has been hard, but I've been sober for a year and a week. I go to meetings and work the program." He is quiet for a moment. "Thank you for being there for my dad. I think our little girl has given him a purpose and he has loved spending time with you."

"It's no hardship spending time with Robert. Dinner will be done soon, why don't you go get some snuggle time with Madison?"

Once he disappears, I'm able to breathe normally. I don't know why I am suddenly feeling hot or why my skin feels too tight. I shake my head and then get back to making dinner.

* * *

I PULL into Abby's driveway, and she comes running out the front door. Shaking my head, I watch my big sister run toward the back door and get her niece out. In a flash she disappears back into the house.

Once I'm inside the house I find my sister getting Madison out of her carrier and snuggling her to her chest.

"Um, hello? I am your sister, remember me?" I cross my arms in a fake pout.

Abby comes toward me and kisses my cheek. "You look good. Is this princess finally sleeping through the night?"

I nod. "The past couple of nights she's slept for six hours straight. It's been fantastic."

"That is such a good feeling. The boys both started sleeping through the night after a month. Paisley was the one that took about six or seven months." Abby sniffs Madison's head. "God, I miss this smell."

I begin to laugh because every woman in my family sniffs my daughter's head. It's the lavender and chamomile body wash I use on her and the lotion. "Lucky for you she's not gassy. That overpowers her sweet baby smell." My daughter is gorgeous but she's got the stinkiest toots and poops.

"Ben and the kids should be home soon," Abby says as she leads me into the kitchen, grabbing me a glass of lemonade—all while holding my daughter. "He wanted to give me a break, so they went to the park."

I smile wide because it makes me happy that my sister has someone who loves her so much and takes care of her when she needs it. "You are one lucky woman. That man would move heaven and earth for you."

Her cheeks turn a deep shade of pink, making me jealous, but in the best way because I want a man who is just like him. "Yes, he would, and I would do the same." Abby hands me a glass. "Have you seen Chris much?" I knew this was coming. He's been home for a week now.

"Pretty much every day that I go to see Robert or when he's got Madison." I take a sip of my lemonade. "Yesterday when I went to pick her up I found Chris and Madison on the floor. She was lying on a little playmat he bought her, and they were having tummy time."

Abby grins at me and then down at my napping daughter. "That makes me glad. He's been sober since he left?"

I nod. "Yeah, he looks good...healthy. Robert is so happy, and that makes me happy."

"What will happen with the two of you?" she asks. My little girl wakes up and kicks her feet when her auntie starts talking to her.

I smile at Madison and grab her foot before looking at Abby. "Nothing will happen. I just hope we can work together co-parenting Madison. Plus, Graham and I have been spending lots of time together and I've been thinking about pursuing something with him." *That's if he's even interested*, I think to myself.

"I could see that. He's sweet and obviously cares about you, and he's smitten with this little angel."

I shrug. "I guess we'll see what happens."

Then her family comes home, and their beautiful chaos ensues.

CHRIS

I lie in bed flipping through all the pictures I've taken over the past week. My daughter is so beautiful I can't stand it. I hate that I was too loaded to remember conceiving her, but that is not me anymore.

My road to recovery this past year has been the hardest thing I've ever gone through, but I am thankful every day that I did it. I've almost relapsed twice and the first time was when I had dreamt of my mom dying. I bought a bottle of whiskey, but then dumped it down the drain.

The second time was right after Madison's birth. Dad had sent me the video of moments after she was born and a picture of my daughter on her mom's chest. She was covered in goo, but she was still the most beautiful baby I've ever seen. I flip to that video and picture and can smile now when I look at it.

I look at Haddie, even though her hair is a mess, and she looks exhausted—I've never seen her look more beautiful. I wasn't sure if she'd let me spend time with Madison, but I am thankful she did.

Also, how do I ever repay her for giving our daughter my

mother's name? I'm sure Mom is looking down on her namesake and is completely in love.

I hear the doorbell and then Dad's bedroom door. I get out of bed, throwing on some sweatpants, and head out to the foyer where Robert, Haddie, and Madison are standing.

That's when I notice my dad looks terrible. His eyes are on Haddie. "I'm so sorry, sweetheart. I should've called you sooner, but I slept through my alarm."

"I'm so sorry you're not feeling well. I'll just take her to my mom's." She smiles at him and then picks up the carrier.

"Why don't I watch her?" I say. "Dad is here if I have questions and if we run into too much trouble, we can call your mom or Abby."

Haddie looks at me and then Madison, and then back up at me. "Yeah, okay. Your dad has the important numbers. She just ate before we left, so she should be good for a few hours. Don't be offended if I call to check in and I may come have lunch here."

"No worries, call as much as you need to." I take the carrier from her. "Dad, you get in bed. Maddie and I are going into the family room to watch cartoons.

Haddie leans down, kissing the baby's forehead, and then looks at my dad. "I'll bring you some medicine and soup later. You get in bed."

She looks at me one more time before leaving. I pick up the diaper bag and turn to Dad. "Go get some rest. Maddie and I will be fine."

He disappears down the hall and I look at my sleeping daughter. "Its just you and me, baby girl." I carry her to the family room and I'm excited to spend the day taking care of my daughter.

* * *

I OPEN my eyes and realize I fell asleep. I smile when I look down, looking at my little girl snoozing on my chest.

Today has been a good day. We had lots of tummy time and she was obsessed with *Cocomelon*. I don't think she knew what she was looking at, but I'm sure she liked the bright colors and the songs.

She had two massive blow outs. One required a bath and an outfit change. I almost freaked out, but I got my shit together and we got through it. I wrap my arms around her to sit up.

Madison squeaks and then scrunches up her body. She looks up at me and the most amazing thing happens, she smiles up at me. "Hey, baby girl. Do you know I'm your daddy?" I kiss the top of her head and hug her to my chest. Fuck, I love her so much.

My stomach aches thinking about how I could've royally screwed this up—well, actually I did royally screw up, but I can't regret something that gave me such a beautiful girl I never knew I needed.

I make sure I have Madison's head supported and push up to a sitting position. I freeze, Haddie is standing in the middle of the family room watching us. "Hey, sorry, I came to check on you guys, and your dad. You guys were sleeping so good, I didn't want to wake you."

"She's like a natural sleeping pill," I tell her.

Haddie nods. "Those are my best naps, when she's on my chest." She holds up a bag. "I brought Robert some chicken noodle soup and us a pizza. I thought I would eat lunch with you, or if you already ate, I'll eat by myself."

I stand up. "I could eat." I grab Madison's bouncy seat and carry it into the kitchen, setting it on the island.

Haddie comes over, taking Madison from my arms and kissing all over her face. "My sweet baby girl. Mommy missed you." The baby gurgles and smiles at Haddie. "Are you having fun with your daddy?"

Man, hearing her call me Daddy to our daughter does something to me. Before I start crying like a pussy, I grab the container of soup and get a spoon. "I-I'm going to take this to Dad."

She kisses the top of Madison's head. "Okay, I'll get us some plates for the pizza."

I nod and then head to Dad's bedroom. I reach the door and knock, when I hear Dad's faint voice, I open the door. I find Dad sitting on the side of his bed. "How are you feeling?"

He shakes his head. "Like shit." My dad has never been a huge curser, and it's funny to hear him do it. "Everything going okay? Where's Madison?"

"Haddie's here. She brought you this." I hold the soup up. "She brought us pizza." I set the soup container down on the nightstand.

Dad smiles up at me. "She's too good to me."

"Do you need anything?" I sit down next to him.

He slaps my shoulder. "No, you should go eat lunch with the girls. I'm going to eat this soup and go back to bed."

"Okay, let me know if you need anything." I stand up and head to the door.

I'm ready to step out, when my dad calls my name. "I'm really glad you're home. I've said it before, and I'll say it again and again. I am so proud of you. Your mom would be too—maybe not how we got here, but how you've grown over this past year."

"Ahem...thanks, Dad. That means a lot." I shut the door behind me and take a second to collect myself.

In the kitchen I find Haddie holding a blanket in front of her face and then pull it down, smiling at our girl. She smiles up at her mom like she's the greatest thing, and from what I've seen she's an amazing mother.

Haddie notices me watching her and her cheeks turn an adorable pink. "She's—um—easily entertained." She leans in, kissing Madison's cheek. "Lets eat." We grab some pizza and sit down at the island. "What are you going to do for work? Are you going back into real estate?"

I wipe my mouth and look toward her. "I have a couple of interviews for some construction work. Honestly, I love it a lot more than I thought I would. There's just something about building something with your own two hands."

"Why don't you apply at my dad and uncles' company. They're always looking for more help."

I know she's just trying to help, but I highly doubt her father or uncles want me anywhere near them. I did write Dylan and JoJo, Haddie and Joe's mom and dad, apologizing for what I did and leaving their youngest daughter pregnant.

They responded, but it was very formal. I deserve it and hate that I've lost my second family. I'm just glad they didn't cut my dad off—Dylan is always taking my dad out to do stuff.

I focus back on Haddie. "I'm not sure they would go for that. Both places looked promising, and I have a killer letter of recommendation from the owner of the company I worked for."

"That's great. I've never seen you so buff." Her cheeks turn red and she turns away from me.

I decide to lighten the mood. "You think I'm buff?" I then flex my muscles, making her laugh. It's a sweet sound that does something to my chest.

We go back to eating, it's a comfortable silence, and it's not lost on me that we're both watching our daughter while we eat.

Haddie's on her third piece when her phone rings. She

picks it up. "Oh, it's work. I need to take this." Once she disappears into the family room, I start straightening up the kitchen.

The baby begins to fuss. "What's wrong, sweet girl?" I quickly pull her out of her bouncy seat and bounce her lightly in my arms.

She rubs her forehead against my chest, making me smile. Haddie comes in. "I've got to get going. I should be back around five."

"We'll be here." She comes up to me and Madison and leans in, kissing our daughter on the head. "Have a good rest of your day," I tell her. She smiles at me and then grabs her backpack, disappearing out of the room. I carry Madison into the family room and while I do some pushups, she watches me with her big blue eyes.

HADDIE

"*D*ad, do you have a second?" I step into his office and shut the door behind me.

He stands and comes around the desk to engulf me in a huge hug. "Of course. Is Madison okay?"

I nod. "Of course, she's with Chloe right now. I just wanted to talk to you about something."

Dad leans against his desk. "Lay it on me."

"I want you to offer Chris a job." Of course, as soon as the words left my mouth, Dad's face turns to stone.

My dad and uncles have the best architecture firm/construction company in all of South Carolina. Hell, half my family works for them, including my cousin Violet and her husband, Diego.

"Why the fuck would I hire a junkie?"

I stand up. "Hey, that's not fair. Addiction is a sickness. Is Abby a junkie?" My sister's drug and alcohol problem were after her assault, and she went into to treatment, just like Chris.

"It's not the same thing. She was self-medicating after

what happened to her." He crosses his arms over his broad chest.

"You don't know why Chris used, but he's sober now and has been for a year. He's also the father of your granddaughter, whether you like it or not. Doesn't he deserve a second chance? People gave Abby one." I sit back down. "He's trying to make amends. Why can't you give him a chance to do that? If not for me, what about for Madison? How will that feel for her, knowing that part of her family doesn't like her dad?"

He doesn't say anything for a bit and then he nods. "You're right, I'm sorry. I'll think about talking to him about a job. That's the best I can do."

I stand up and wrap my arms around him. "That's all I ask." He leads me down to the offices of my uncles, Dustin and Luke, and Violet and Diego's.

After saying hello to everyone, I head out to Joe and Chloe's. My sister-in-law is watching my daughter. I pull into their driveway and climb out. Not bothering to knock, I step inside. "Hello?" I call out.

My nephew spots me and comes running on his little chubby legs. "Ha!" he shouts. I scoop him up into my arms, making him giggle as I kiss his neck.

"How's my boy?" He smiles up at me and it's amazing how much he looks like my brother. "Where's Momma?"

He babbles in his baby language as we walk into the living room where Chloe is sitting on the floor with my daughter in her lap. JJ runs to his mom and wraps his arms around her neck, pulling her to him for a smooch. She smiles up at me, looking like a tatted-up version of Snow White. "Hey you."

I sit down on the floor, grabbing my nephew, and pulling him down to my lap. "How was she?" Madison stares at JJ like she doesn't know what to think of him. He's a good boy, he's just a wild man.

"Great, of course. Ragnar and Lagertha kept watch while

she took a nap." Those are Chloe's Maine Coon cats. They're huge, but so cute, and so sweet. "That one has been a little jealous of Miss Madison here."

"Uh oh." I kiss the top of JJ's head.

"It wasn't bad, he just wanted in my lap every time I've held her." She looks me over closely. "How are things now that Chris is home?"

This is probably my brother, Joe, asking, but maybe if they know things are going well between us maybe it might help bridge the gap between my brother and his best friend. "Good, awkward. He's really good with Madison."

I grab my phone and open the picture app. "I took this the other day." I show Chloe the picture I took when I found Madison asleep on Chris's chest. He was sleeping too and was holding her to his chest—it warmed my heart.

Chloe looks at it and smiles. "That is so sweet. He's laying down, but he looks good, healthy."

"He really does. There is just a more relaxed vibe around him." I hug JJ. "He is truly trying to make things right. He loves our little girl so much."

She nods. "That makes me glad, sweetheart." Chloe is quiet for a moment and then looks at me. "He's tried to talk to Joe, but your brother is just not ready."

My stomach tightens and my chest hurts. "I-I get it, I do. He's a different person, Chloe."

She looks me over closely. "Do you have feelings for him?"

I shake my head. "No, not at all. We were barely friends when we...you know. I just think back to when Abby went through everything, and no one batted an eye about forgiving her and bringing her back into the fold. Chris is Madison's father and he's going to be in our lives. My daughter should be able to have her whole family together to celebrate the events in her life, without excluding anyone."

Chloe bends down, kissing Madison on the top of the head. "You're right. I'll talk to Joe."

"Thank you."

We head out after that, and when I get back to my apartment, I get Little Miss Thang out and carry her toward the stairs.

"Well hey, you two." Lance says from his open door. He's been so great about not being loud when we're home. Hell, he's even helped me get her upstairs if I have a lot of bags and stuff to carry.

"Hey Lance." He gives me a salute before lighting up a cigarette and sitting down on the little bench outside of his door. Once I'm up the stairs, I open the apartment door and set the baby carrier down on the living room floor.

I kick my shoes off and drop my bag on the sofa. Madison is kicking her feet and cooing. I never really wanted kids, but I already can't imagine my life without her. I pluck her out of the carrier and kiss her. "What should we do tonight? Should we watch a movie? Maybe go out dancing?"

She coos and smiles at me. I lay her down on her activity mat and turn the music on. Madison kicks her legs and waves her arms while she watches the little light show.

I hurry into the kitchen and decide on a peanut butter and jelly sandwich for dinner. While I eat, I nurse Madison, and we watch *Supernatural* on Netflix. Once I finish my sandwich, I grab her soft little hand and hold onto it while she finishes eating.

My phone pings with an incoming text.

Graham: Hey, I'm outside and have ice cream.

I smile and stand up with Madison still attached to my breast. He's seen me feed her before, I'm not shy about it because it's completely natural. I open the door and he doesn't even look at my boob hanging out. "Hey, come on in."

"We haven't seen each other in over a week. I figure we're

due for a catch up." I step back so he can walk in. He kisses my cheek as he steps inside.

Madison finishes up and when Graham comes back in from the kitchen, I'm burping her. "So what's going on?" he says as he plops down on the sofa.

"Has it really been a week since we talked?" He nods. "I'm sorry, it's just been so crazy. Chris is back."

Graham's eyes widen. "Chris? Madison's dad, Chris?"

I nod. "Yep, one and the same. He's staying with his dad right now."

"How did it go when he saw her?" He holds out his hands and I hand my daughter over to him. She loves her Graham and snuggles into his chest.

"It was great. He was gaga for her, and she was gaga for him. It was pretty sweet."

I get up and grab us two bowls of ice cream. Graham takes his and places it on the coffee table. Madison's falling asleep on his shoulder as he pats her back. This is about her bedtime.

"I'm going to change her and then lay her down. I'll be right back." He kisses her forehead and then hands her to me.

Once I lay her down in the crib a few minutes later, I lean down, kissing her cheek. I whisper, "I love you, my sweet baby girl." Her pacifier moves as she sucks on it and she looks up at me with her blue eyes.

It doesn't take long before her eyes flutter shut. I grab the baby monitor off the charger, turning it on. She appears on the little screen, and I head out to the living room.

Graham looks up when I step back into the room. I sit on the sofa with my legs tucked under me and begin to eat my ice cream. "How are your classes this semester?" He has one more year and he'll have his degree in criminal justice.

"Easy. I wish I were done already. I want to be a cop so damn bad."

I laugh as he shoves a huge spoonful into his mouth. "You're such a pig."

"Oink, oink, baby." Graham then snorts like a pig. "Tell me about your week."

I take the last bite and then set the bowl down. "It's been interesting. I didn't know Chris was back until the day I showed up to see Robert."

"Is it a good thing he's back?"

I nod, slowly. "It is, especially for Robert and Madison." I shrug. "I hold no ill-will toward him. He didn't force me; I gave it up easily to him. Yes, it's unfortunate that things fell apart for him, but he's Madison's father. If he's sober, and wants to spend time with her, he can."

"You're so wise for someone who's only twenty."

I shake with laughter. He's always telling me that I'm an old soul and I interpret that as being totally lame. "That's me, I'm a regular Obi-Wan Kenobi."

He throws a pillow at me. "You're such a dork."

I come over and sit next to him, with my head on his shoulder. "What about you? Is everything going okay?"

"It is. You know me, just school and work. I've missed you." He kisses my forehead. "How's work?"

"Good, I'm still on a modified orientation. All that means is I have a smaller case load, but every week they're adding more." I like that they haven't just thrown me into it, they've taken the time to teach me right.

"That's because you're a kick ass nurse." He's quiet for a second. "I wanted to talk to you about something."

Oh God, is he going to ask me out? I honestly don't think I'll ever see him as anything other than a friend—I've hoped and hoped feelings would develop for him, but they just haven't. I hold my breath and wait for him to say whatever it is he's going to say, while trying to figure out to let him down easy. "Okay, what's going on?"

"I-I've met someone. It's still very new, but I really like him," Graham says that last part quietly.

I sit up. "Him? Oh my god, why didn't you tell me? I thought you were going to ask me out." I wrap my arms around him. "This is great news, I'm happy for you."

Graham shakes his head. "I wanted to tell you so many times, but I'd chicken out. I'm sorry I didn't tell you sooner."

"No, don't apologize. That is your journey—your life, and you tell me when you're ready." I snuggle into his side. It fills me with so much love for him to know he trusts me with is heart. I feel really lucky.

We sit snuggled together and he tells me all about Casey, the man who is making him blush.

CHRIS

y feet slap against the road as I jog around my neighborhood. I've been home for two weeks now and it's been good. Haddie has let me spend as much time with Madison as I want. I've never loved someone the way I love my little girl already.

I can't help but smile as I think of Madison. Yesterday when we watched her while Haddie worked, she was on her little mat, doing some tummy time. I was lying on my stomach in front of her, doing pushups, and she did the sweetest thing.

She began "talking" to me while smiling and pushing up on her arms. We did it until her little arms couldn't hold her up anymore. Dad sat in his recliner, smiling as he watched us.

Thankfully he is feeling better, but I've asked him to be more hands on with my daughter. He laughed his ass off earlier when my beautiful little girl shit up her back and up her front, smiling while she did it. Dad laughed even harder while I gagged over and over. It put the last blowout she had to shame.

I learned real quick that a quick spray in the tub is perfect for cleaning a baby covered in shit that no baby wipe could help. She kicked her arms and legs as she laid on the floor, wrapped in her towel. It took me a bit to get her all dried off, diapered, lotioned, and dressed.

After a half hour I head toward home. I hate not working, but hopefully I'll hear from one of the construction crews I interviewed with yesterday.

They're both supervisor positions, but I made it known that I have no problem jumping in where needed. One thing I've learned is I love working with my hands. Who knew that manual labor would be what I'm good at?

I reach my street and find a big ass red truck in the driveway. I'm not sure who it could be.

Stepping inside, I kick off my shoes, and as I head toward the family room, I hear a couple of male voices. The closer I get, the more I recognize the voice. I stop just short of the entryway and take a deep breath. I'm nervous about seeing him.

"Hey," I say as I step into the room.

Dylan surprises me as he stands up with my daughter in his arm. "Welcome home. It looks like California did wonders for you."

I nod. "Yeah, thanks. I think so too." Reaching out, I stroke Madison's cheek. She grabs my finger, trying to pull it to her mouth. "No, no, baby. I need to shower." I kiss her hand and then back away "I'll be back, I just want to shower quick."

"Wait. Chris, do you have a second?" Dylan hands Madison off to Dad.

I lead him to the French doors, and we step onto the deck. "What's going on?" I'm almost afraid of what he's going to say.

"I heard that you were doing some construction in California."

"Yeah, I started out as a grunt, and found out I had a natural skill in carpentry. I've discovered that I love working with my hands." I place my hands on my hips. I'm not sure what he's saying, but I wish he'd spit it out.

"We have a new project we're taking on and I think you might be able to help in two ways. We're going to start buying houses, remodeling them, and then selling them. If you're interested, we could use your carpentry skills and your real estate expertise."

I rock back on my heels. "Why me?"

"I heard you might be looking for work, and your dad got me the letter of recommendation your boss wrote you. I think you'd be a great fit."

As good as it sounds, this feels like Haddie. "Did Haddie ask you to do this?"

He shrugs. "She may have mentioned that you were looking for work."

My stomach turns and disappointment fills me. "I'm good. I've got a couple of interviews I'm waiting to hear back from. With all due respect, I don't want a pity job." They told me in treatment that repairing relationships was going to take work, and some may not be salvageable.

I guess I'm just embarrassed about what I turned into. I'd hate for my daughter to ever find out her dad was an addict and just about ruined his life. Fuck, I need to stop with the pity party. If I take the job, I'll prove to them that they did right, by hiring me.

"Listen, I admit at first I only thought about it because my daughter asked me to, and the fact that you're the father of my granddaughter—after talking to your boss in California, I knew exactly where we could use you. You were a good real-tor, and it makes sense that you could help sell them once they're finished."

I know I should tell him no, that this is a bad idea, but this is a good opportunity for me. I can get some experience and they have a pretty well-known construction company. This could be a good starting point for me.

"Why don't you stop at the office tomorrow around noon and we'll go over everything. Then you can make your decision."

I nod. "Yeah, okay." I stick out my hand. "Thank you for the opportunity."

We step back inside and Dylan steps back into the family room, talking to Dad. I holler as I walk by, "I'm going to take a quick shower."

I head into my bedroom and strip out of my clothes, then hop in the shower.

Once I'm finished, I grab my towel and drying myself off. In my bedroom, I sit down on the side of my bed and grab my phone. I pull up Haddie's phone number.

Chris: Hey, tonight can I come over so we can talk?

I stare down at my phone as the little dots start bouncing. I know she's working, but hopefully I caught her between patients.

Haddie: Sure, is everything okay?

Chris: Yes, of course. Sorry I should've said that first.

Haddie: No worries, I'll text you my address and then just text me when you're coming.

I have time to think about what I want to say, so I stand up and get dressed.

* * *

99

I PULL into the parking space right next to Haddie's car and climb out. I'm not sure what I want to say to her. I was gone earlier when she came to pick up Madison.

I climb up the stairs and pause in front of her door. I'm nervous but I don't really know why. I quickly knock before I turn on my heels and leave. The door opens and there she is, looking beautiful in a pair of cut off sweats and a red t-shirt that hugs her willowy frame. "Hey," she says as she steps backs so I can come inside.

Her place is small but cute. She'll definitely need more space as Madison gets older. On the wall are some photos of Madison as a newborn. She's so beautiful. There's another picture of all the kids in the family. Damn, there are a lot of babies.

"We did the picture for all the grandparents," Haddie says as she stands next to me. "That poor photographer didn't know what she was getting herself into. The older kids helped with the little ones, but it was still chaos."

"I can imagine." I lean in, looking at the kids. "It is not hard to tell which one is JJ. He looks just like Joe."

My heart fucking hurts thinking about Joe. I've tried reaching out and have sent him a few letters, but he hasn't responded. Besides not remembering sleeping with Haddie, hurting Joe is one of my biggest regrets.

"Yes, he does, he acts like him too. It's hilarious watching him." She places her hand on my forearm. "He just needs time."

I shake my head. "I think I burned that bridge." I turn to face her. "Did you tell your dad to give me a job?" She bites her lip and I know immediately that she did. My stomach sinks and I'm not sure I want to take it. "Why?"

"Because their company is the best, I knew you were looking, and I wanted to help."

"Okay, but what made you want to do that for me?"

Haddie steps toward me so we're almost touching. "You're Madison's father, I care about you."

"Thank you," I say softly. "I'm meeting with your dad tomorrow. If I take it, I'll prove to him that I deserve my place."

She smiles up at me. "I don't doubt you will."

I place my hands on her shoulders. "I know you were trying to help, but from now on, let me find my own way."

"Okay." Haddie takes a step back and grabs my hand. "Come on, let's go peek in on Madison."

"Won't we wake her?" I ask in a whisper.

She smiles while shaking her head. "She has a full belly and a clean diaper."

There's a speaker on the dresser, glowing a light blue and playing what sounds like rain showers. We head across the room to the crib that sits against the wall.

I smile when I look down at my sleeping daughter. Her arms are above her head and her pacifier moves as she sucks it in her sleep. "Can I touch her?" I whisper. Haddie nods, so I reach down and stroke a hand over her head. I then rub my hand over her belly.

We leave the room and make our way back into the living room. "I know it's only been a couple of weeks, but you're so good with her," she says.

My throat is suddenly tight and my eyes burn. "I've-I've failed at so many things. I don't want to fail at this."

She grabs my face. "Listen to me. You're going to make mistakes. I've already made mistakes and will probably make some more. We learn from them and hopefully not do them again. Stop worrying, okay? I just remind myself that every mistake I make now, she won't remember."

"Thank you for letting me know her." A tear slips from my eye, since I quick drinking and using I'm a lot more emotional.

She wraps her arms around me, hugging me tight. In turn I wrap my arms around her. We stay locked in an embrace until I feel her yawn. "You should get some sleep. I'll see you tomorrow."

Haddie walks me to the door. "See you tomorrow, Chris." I stand outside and wait until I hear the deadbolt engage before I head back to Dad's.

"Mrs. Johnson, I'll be back in the morning. Just remember we have nurses on call, so if you need anything for Mr. Johnson, don't hesitate to contact them." I pull the magnet out of the admission packet and show it to her. "This is the number you can call."

She takes it from me and nods. "Thank you, Haddie."

I head back to the office to work on my admission and send off orders to the doctor. Once I get that finished, I go see my last two patients for the day. It's been a few days since Chris was over.

The day I talked to my dad I was sure he wouldn't talk to Chris about a job, but was pleasantly surprised to hear that he did. Over the past year, Robert has shown me the work Chris was doing.

He's talented at woodworking and some of the homes he's worked on have been gorgeous. His dad told me that Chris's boss didn't want to lose him and offered him a lot of money to stay.

I'm glad Chris decided to come home, though. He wants to know his daughter and she deserves to know him. Sure, he could've known her living somewhere else, but this will be better for the two of them.

The rest of my workday goes well, and by the time I head to Robert's I am exhausted. Madison decided she was ready to party at four o'clock this morning. Hopefully she'll sleep well tonight and give momma a break.

I pull into the driveway and pop a piece of gum into my mouth. Not bothering to knock, I open the door and call out. "Hello?"

"Back here, sweetheart," Robert answers.

In the family room I find my girl lying on the floor on her tummy, gurgling and babbling at her daddy, who is lying on his stomach in front of her.

"Hi sweetheart, how was your day?" Robert gives me a cheek kiss.

Chris pops up and I ignore the fact that he's in gray sweatpants and no shirt, or at least I try, because it's making me feel all warm inside. I try to ignore him, but it's hard when he bends down to pick up Madison and carries her to me.

"Look, it's Mommy," he says in a soft voice before handing me Madison.

I kiss her cheek. "Hi, sweetheart. I missed you today. Were you a good girl for Daddy and Grandpa?"

"She was perfect," Chris says with a smile. "Maddie did puke in my mouth today, didn't you?" He strokes a hand over her head.

"I told him not to lift her in the air right after her bottle, but someone didn't listen," Robert says with a laugh.

I hug her to my chest. "Naughty girl, puking on Daddy." She wraps her teeny tiny hand around my braid that hangs over my shoulder. Madison grips it tightly and tries to pull it into her mouth. "No, no, baby." I look at Robert. "What should I make for dinner? I think I pulled out some ground beef—I could make a meatloaf."

Robert looks at Chris, and he looks at me. "Dad and I decided we're going to make you dinner tonight. You've done so much, taking care of this old man. Go relax and we're going to cook." Chris gives me a smile and motions for me to get.

In the family room, I curl up in the corner of the sectional. Madison starts nuzzling at my breast. I get myself situated and she latches on immediately. She holds onto my finger as we watch each other.

It's moments like these that I treasure. The love I feel for her is stronger than anything I've felt in my entire life. When I was pregnant with her, I was scared I wouldn't be able to love her, but the second she was in my arms I knew I'd love her until the day I die.

I look up and am startled. Chris is standing in the entry of the family room, watching us. On silent feet he walks toward me and my heart beats wildly in my chest.

He sits down next to me and strokes a hand over Madison's head. "She looks like you." Chris smiles at me and then looks back down at the baby. "I start my job Monday. I'm going to miss seeing her every day."

"You know where I live, you can come see her whenever you want." Madison stops nursing and I pull her from my breast and hand her to Chris to burp while I tuck myself back in. "You're going to do great; you know that, right?"

Chris shakes his head. "I don't understand how you can be so sure after everything that's happened."

"You were the one who decided to go into rehab. *You* decided to stay in California to work on yourself. No one else made *you* do it. I've only done clinicals in the rehab unit at Lutheran, but I know how hard it is. I mean, let's face it, you look really good."

He throws his head back, laughing, and it's a glorious sound. Chris holds onto Madison, and she looks up at him like he's crazy. "T-Thanks," he said with a laugh and then sobers. "How the hell are you so wise?"

"I'm not," I say while shaking my head. "It's just a feeling I have."

His eyes turn bright. "Ahem...well, thank you." Chris leans down, kissing the top of Madison's head, but I can see he's smiling.

* * *

Robert

I WATCH Chris and Haddie from the entry of the family room. They have no clue I'm standing in the same room with them and it makes my heart happy.

This past year I worried so much about my son. First, would he make it through rehab. Next, would he stay sober, and lastly, would I get my son back. As I watch him now, I know my boy is coming back to me.

Madison stares up at her dad with those big blue eyes and you can just tell she loves him so much. I've been leaving him in charge while I run errands and go to the office, mainly to give them the chance to bond. He's certainly becoming a pro at changing diapers and giving baths. It has been wonderful watching my son and granddaughter grow closer.

I only wish my Madison was here to witness our son become a father—to watch him become the man I know he's capable of. God, I miss her—I miss her so much, and hate that she's not here to love on her namesake. That baby girl would be so spoiled and so loved.

I am getting ready to step back when I freeze. Haddie says something to him, and my son throws his head back and laughs, and it's a laugh I haven't heard in a long time.

She smiles at him, and her cheeks turn pink while Madison stares at them both like she doesn't know what they're doing. My boy is happy, which makes me happy. I head back to the kitchen and get out the burgers, seasoning them.

My son joins me a minute later. "Hey, Dad, what do you need from me?"

"Why don't you season the burgers? I'll get the grill going." My son heads back into the house and I head to the grill.

Once the flame is going, I head inside to my family.

CHRIS

I take a drink of my water and then wipe my forehead with the back of my arm. After one more drink I head back over to the sawhorse, stick in my ear plugs, pick up my safety goggles, and place them over my eyes. I use the circular saw to cut the wood for the stairs we're redoing.

I've been working for Carter and Carmichael's for two weeks and I'd love to say it has been great, but truth is, Dylan is always watching me—if not him, it's someone else from Haddie's family. I get it, I do, but if she can forgive me, why can't they?

I know I'll have to earn their trust and I plan on it, but will I ever be accepted? Hell, the only reason I'm here now is because I'm the father of his granddaughter.

Fuck, I miss my girl. I hate that I'm not there for us to have our tummy time.

I'd lay on my stomach, and we'd be face to face. I'd talk to her until she'd start kicking her legs and smiling at me. I loved our morning snuggles. In the recliner I'd be kicked back with her snoozing on my chest.

I haven't seen Madison or Haddie much the past couple

of weeks. I've been working ten to twelve hours a day, wanting to prove my worth to the others. I'm so exhausted when I get home, I usually inhale whatever Haddie made for dinner, shower, and then pass out.

Truth be told, I miss Haddie—I miss her sweet smiles, her soft voice when she talks to our girl, or the way she blushes sometimes when I talk to her. When she bites her lip, I get these flashes of being between her legs, and this intense pleasure.

I focus on my job, not needing to hurt myself. Once I finish with this batch, most of the other guys are back from lunch. They've all been friendly enough, but knowing I need to prove myself. I just keep my head down and work.

At quitting time, I take off my tool belt and toss it to the side as I help put everything away. I finish up and grab my stuff and head outside to my truck. "Chris." I stop and turn to find Violet, Haddie's cousin, walking toward me.

"Hey, did you need something?" I turn to face her fully.

She shakes her head. "No, well—I just wanted to welcome you to the crew. I know things are weird, but I just wanted you to know that we've been so pleased with your work." Violet shakes her head. "You're talented." She shrugs. "I just wanted to let you know that."

I watch her walk away and I'm sure my mouth is hanging open. I've been working with her and her husband Diego's team, which surprised me. I thought Dylan would want me to be with him so he could watch me like a hawk.

Once I become unstuck, I head to much truck—I never thought I'd be a truck man, but once I saw how much easier it was to haul stuff around, I had Dad sell my BMW and he wired me the money. I bought my black Toyota Tundra and I haven't looked back.

At home, I find Haddie's car in the driveway and my heart does this weird little skip. Although I'm fucking exhausted, I practically jog into the house. Inside, I quickly take off my steel-toed boots and hustle into my room to shower. It takes a few minutes and then I pop out, dry off, and throw on some shorts and a t-shirt.

In the family room I find Dad and Haddie are sitting on the sofa watching Madison play in the exersaucer I bought for her.

"Hi, baby girl," I say, and she immediately looks my way and smiles. My heart swells and my eyes burn. This little girl has my heart and she doesn't know it. I get down on the floor, and kiss her forehead. She bounces a little and starts gurgle talking to me.

I stand up. "Hey, you two," I say as I sit in the recliner.

"How was work?" Dad asks as he stands up.

"Busy, but good. I've been working on the staircase. Wait until you see it, I think it's going to be amazing." I grab my phone and pull up the picture I took of my progress.

"Oh my god, that's so cool," Haddie gushes as she looks at the picture. "Look at that detail."

My chest puffs with pride, but then someone doesn't like being ignored. Madison lets out a screech and I turn around to grab her out of the toy. She rests her forehead against my neck and rubs it back and forth.

I turn back to the two of them while I snuggle my girl. "What are you guys thinking for dinner?"

"What about ordering pizza?" Haddie stands up. "You two can have whatever leftovers there are and take it for lunch."

Dad orders the pizza and breadsticks, then heads down the hall to his office to do some work. Haddie and I sit on the floor with our legs in a V and our feet touching. Madison sits between my legs and I have one arm wrapped around her, and with the other Haddie and I roll a ball that lights up and plays music.

A couple of times our girl gets so excited and tries to

lunge for it, but luckily, I have a firm hold on her. Haddie's soft laughter does something to my chest, but it seems to happen every time I'm around her.

"How do you like being a nurse?" Fuck, I'm dumb.

She smiles and then tucks her hair behind her ear. "I love it. I actually love it more than I thought I would. I mean it's hard, but I'm making a difference and helping people through the end of their life."

"That's really great." I stand up with Madison and kiss the top of her head.

After pizza and breadsticks, I help Haddie get the baby loaded up in her car. Once the car seat is snapped in place, I kiss my sleeping daughter. I shut the door and stand to my full height.

I cover my mouth as I yawn—that's one thing about my job, I'm freaking exhausted every night when I get home. The only bad part of that is I haven't been to a meeting since I started, but I need to get to one.

"Go inside and go to bed," Haddie says as she smiles up at me. "Mom's got Madison tomorrow since your dad's in court all day, but you're always welcome to come over if you want."

I nod. "Okay, I'll text you." I stand on the driveway and watch her back out, give me a wave, and then pull away. As soon as the taillights disappear into the night, I head inside.

* * *

I step out of the little Baptist church, after my NA meeting, and make my way toward my truck, but freeze—across the street are Joe and Chloe, their son in his arms. Surprisingly, Chloe smiles and jogs across the street toward me. "Hey Chris. How are you?" I'm shocked when she wraps her arms around me.

"I—um—I'm good. Congrats on your boy. He looks like

Joe," I tell her and notice Joe walking slowly across the street toward us.

"He does, and he acts like him too," she says with a laugh. "He keeps us on our toes. How are Haddie and Madison? We haven't seen much of her lately."

Is Chloe fishing for information? Joe comes and stands next to his wife, but doesn't say anything to me. I can't worry about him right now. There is a lot that needs to be said, but not here, not now.

"They're good. Madison is really starting to recognize my voice and smiles at me. It has done wonders for Dad to take care of her." Sure, he gets sad and still misses my mom terribly, but his granddaughter has eased something in his broken heart.

"That's great. He was definitely the proud grandpa when she was born, passing out cigars to everyone he saw." That makes me happy. "You haven't officially met, but this is JJ." She grabs the baby boy's foot, shaking it.

I reach out my hand, grabbing his, and give it a shake. "What's up, little dude?" He gives me a toothy, drooly smile. "He's a good looking boy," I say, looking at Joe, who shows no reaction whatsoever. I sound like a chick, but it fucking kills me.

"He sure is," Chloe says and gives me a genuine smile.

We all stand on the sidewalk, looking at each other, and it's awkward. I decide I'll be nice and give them an out. I grab my phone, pretending to look at it. "I've got to get going. I think Dad wanted to go have dinner, but it was good seeing you."

"Yeah, bye, Chris," she says.

I watch them cross the street, and then climb in my truck. I stop by Starbucks and grab a coffee, then take it to the river where I sit and chain smoke. Joe and I were like brothers— fuck, no, we were brothers.

We did everything together, but then I fucked it all up. He can't expect me to regret it though, because if it hadn't happened then we wouldn't have Madison. I wish I remembered that night, but I can't go back and change anything.

That was one thing I learned in rehab, that I couldn't change what put me there. I needed to just look forward, not back. It is obviously easier said than done. My phone pings and I see it's a text from Haddie.

I open it and immediately smile. It's a picture of Madison wrapped in a towel, smiling a toothless smile. I read the text.

Haddie: Someone just had a bath and wanted to say "night night Daddy."

I type out a quick text to her.

Chris: Tell her I said "goodnight baby" and that I love her.

My phone dings and it's another picture, but this time it's Madison in Haddie's arms and their faces are pressed together. Madison looks adorable and when I look at Haddie I realize just how beautiful she truly is. I mean, she was cute when she was a kid, but now as a woman, she's fucking stunning. If our daughter looks anything like her, she's never dating...ever.

I don't know if she's applying for sainthood, but I don't deserve to have her in my life. I still don't understand why she's my biggest cheerleader after what I did to her. I'm just thankful she's letting me be part of Madison's life.

HADDIE

"*W*hy did I let you talk me into this?" I glare at my big sister, and she just laughs her ass off.

She got me to do this stupid ass Crossfit again, and I must've blocked out how hard it was last time. At least I didn't collapse on the mat this time. I use the hand towel Abby brought for me to wipe the sweat pouring down my face. She hands me a bottle of water and I slam it down.

"You know, it really sucks that you have a perfect mode-lesque body," she says as she looks me over.

I shake my head. "What are you talking about? I'm built like a boy. You're the one with the smokin' hot body." My sister has always been beautiful, and now that she's happily married and has four beautiful children, she is always freaking glowing.

Don't get me wrong, she and Ben fight and the kids drive her crazy, but after what she went through, she deserves to glow.

"You are not built like a boy. You're built like Giselle." We make our way to her minivan and climb inside. "How is

Chris doing? I saw him the other day at the grocery store, and he looks good."

I don't want to admit that I've definitely noticed how good he looks; he's tan, built, and bright eyed—so different from the guy I saw the day I told him I was pregnant. I am not going to tell Abby I'm extremely attracted to him and that sometimes I just want to jump him.

"Oh my God, you like him," she squeals.

My cheeks immediately burn, turning bright red—I'm sure. "Noooo…I do not." I cover my face as I squeal. "I don't, I can't."

"Honey, why can't you?" She pulls my hands from my face.

I shrug. "I don't know, it would complicate things. Plus, I don't think he'd ever really be into me." I look down at my lap.

"You like him," Abby says softly.

"Ugh…I do. I watch him with Madison and he's so good with her. She loves him so much already, and when she hears his voice—she'll look around for him. Then when I'm there we hang out and talk. He'll tuck my hair behind my ear or touch my arm and I don't know. I just look forward to seeing him." I close my eyes and rest my head against the headrest.

"Of course, she loves her daddy, and you—well, he'd be crazy not to see what a catch you are, but I do think you should be cautious. I haven't used in a really long time, but that doesn't mean that every now and then I don't think about it." My eyes widen. "You know what I do, I call Cash." That's Abby's biological dad. "He's been sober a very long time and he knows what I need to hear, and then it passes and I tell Ben."

I shake my head. "Okay, but what are you saying?"

Abby smiles at me. "I just want you to make sure you're going to be able to stay strong when he gets the urge to use, because he will, and that's not saying anything bad about him, it's just the truth."

"I get what you're saying. I'm not sure he thinks of me as anything more than Madison's mom."

Abby gives me a smile. "We'll see." Luckily, she doesn't say anything else about it.

We get back to her house and when we step inside, I find my niece Natalie holding Madison while sitting next to her dad. They smile and I notice little Pay Pay is standing next to her big sister's legs, holding her cousin's hand. "Hey guys. How was she?"

Ben stands and kisses the top of my head before wrapping his arm around my sister. "She was perfect. She and the girls had tummy time while the boys destroyed their room."

"Well, thank you for watching her. I appreciate it." I smile up at him.

He kisses my sister and then smiles at me. "I like getting my baby fix, and since we're done having babies…" He pouts. "I'll have to get my baby snuggles where I can."

"Uh…I think four children are enough." Abby looks at me. "He wouldn't care if I wanted four more."

Ben shrugs. "Hey, we make pretty great kids."

They help me get Madison in her carrier and walk me out. "I'll talk to you two lovebirds later."

On my way home, my phone rings and on the display, I see it's Graham. "Hey you. How's it going?"

"Hey beautiful. I wanted to see if you wanted to grab lunch." My stomach growls immediately and his laugh comes through the phone. "I'll take that as a yes."

"Yes, definitely. I'll warn you, I just got done doing Crossfit with Abby, so I'm gross."

"Not possible. Do you want to meet at the little diner on Main?" Graham says, as I turn on my blinker to turn and head toward Main.

I nod, even though he can't see me. "Yep, we're heading there now."

"Sweet, I'll see you in a few." He disconnects and my music comes back on.

"Madison, we're meeting Uncle Graham for lunch," I announce to my girl, who has no clue what I said, but I talk to her anyway. She gurgles in response, and I smile. I find a spot to park right on Main Street.

I slip on my backpack and then grab Madison's carrier out of the backseat. I step inside and Graham is already here. He waves at me from his booth, standing up as I approach. "Give me that baby."

I hand the carrier over to him and he kisses my cheek. He sets the carrier in the booth as I sit down and quickly undoes her harness, picking her up. "There is my beautiful girl." Graham kisses her head and baby girl smiles up at him. "How are things going?"

Our waitress interrupts us to take our drink order, and once she leaves, I answer him. "We're good. Just work and taking care of baby girl. I did Crossfit with Abby today and I feel like Jell-O."

He starts to laugh and shakes his head. "You are such a wuss." Graham holds up Madison, so they're eye to eye. "Is Mommy a wuss?"

The little booger gurgles at him, making him smile. "Quit telling my daughter lies."

The waitress comes back with drinks and takes our order.

"Tell me, what's going on with you and Casey?" I still haven't met the guy he's dating or whatever is going on.

He smiles softly. "We're still just talking. He's uncomfortable with the fact that I'm bi." Graham kisses the top of Madison's head. "We'll see what happens."

"Before you told me about Casey, I thought you were

going to ask me out. I told myself to say yes, even though I think of you as more of a best friend," I tell him and shrug.

"Oh, I was interested in you at first. You were clearly not into me, but there was just something that made me want to at least be your friend."

I've never been uber emotional, but Graham's going to make me cry. "You are an amazing guy."

Our food comes and he places Madison in the carrier. "Well, you're an amazing woman." He looks down at the baby. "You are too, sweet girl."

While we eat we talk about work and school, and luckily he hasn't asked me about Chris. Abby's talk earlier has me so confused. The more I get to know him, the more I see what a good man he truly is. I don't think he sees it, but he is so strong.

"Hey." I blink and then focus on Graham. "Are you okay? Your face went blank."

"I'm sorry, my mind was wandering. I'm just tired." He looks at me with a furrowed brow and then nods. "Madison was up early and then that damn Crossfit workout kicked my ass." I hold up my hands. "I'm good, I promise."

We finish lunch and he refuses to let me pay. He straps my daughter in, and we climb out of the booth. Graham carries Madison as we walk through the diner. We're almost to the door when I freeze.

Chris is sitting in a booth by the entrance and he's across from a gorgeous redhead. He sees me and he holds my gaze. My stomach twists as she looks me up and down, obviously sizing me up.

I hear my baby girl gurgle from her carrier and become unstuck. On quick feet, I hustle toward the door. I take Madison from Graham.

"What's going on, Haddie? You look spooked." He follows me to my car.

"N-Nothing. I just am not feeling well." I quickly get her loaded up and climb in. "I'll call you later."

I pull away from the curb and head toward home. By the time I pull into the parking lot, I'm hurt, and I know I have no right to be, but I still am. While still sitting in my car, I call my mom.

"Hey, honey. How are you?"

"Hi, Mom. Can I come over? Can Madison and I spend the night?" I try to keep my voice casual, but Mom knows me better.

"Of course. I'll set up the playpen in your old room. Daddy can handle Madison and then you and I are going to sit outside, drink some wine, and you're going to tell me what has you upset. See you soon." That crazy woman hangs up on me. I decide to take her over to Mom and Dad's now, and I'll come back to pack our bag by myself.

The moment we pull into my parents' driveway, Dad is at the backdoor getting Madison out. "There's Papa's girl."

My daughter coos at her Papa as I climb out and follow them inside. "Hey Dad, remember me?"

He turns around and laughs. "Sorry, sweetheart. I was excited to hear my babies were spending the night with us tonight." Dad kisses my cheek and then unhooks Madison from the carrier and they disappear into the family room, where all of the grandkids' stuff is.

Mom is in the kitchen, pulling some cupcakes out of the oven. "Hey, baby." She opens her arms and I step right into them, hugging my mom tight.

"Hey, Mom. Thanks for letting us stay over. I hope we're not going to be cramping your style."

She wraps her arm around my waist. "Never. I haven't seen you much lately. It'll be nice to spend the evening with my baby."

"I'm going to run home quick to pack a bag and shower. Dad has Madison."

Mom gives me a squeeze. "Sure thing, take your time. We've got that little angel."

I head out and climb in my car. I pull out of the driveway and head home.

HADDIE

I step out of the shower, wrap my hair in a towel, and throw on my robe. I grab my lotion and rub it in. In the bathroom I take the towel off my head and comb out my hair and then quickly braid the wet curls.

There's a knock on my door. I head through the apartment and look out the peephole. I close my eyes and debate on answering the door.

"Please open the door, Haddie," Chris says from the other side of the door.

I take a deep breath, plaster a fake smile on my face. "Hey, what are you doing here?" I am so proud of my performance.

He looks down at my body and I realize I'm in my robe—did I forget to mention that it's really short and I'm naked underneath it? He grabs my hand and steps through my door, shutting it behind him. "Go put some clothes on, babe. I'll wait out here."

I just stand in front of him like an idiot. He smiles and then chuckles, and that unfreezes me. I narrow my eyes at him and then hustle back into my bedroom. After throwing on a tank top and knit shorts, I slowly make my way back into the living room where Chris is standing where I left him.

"Who was the guy you were with at the diner?" His question surprises me.

I cross my arms. "Who was the redhead?"

"That was Cherie. She was my boss when I was working in realty. I wanted to prove to your dad and everyone else that I'm an asset. I figured if I met with her and worked out a deal to buy houses and then selling them once they're flipped, that it would be another way I could contribute."

I shake my head. "You don't have to explain yourself to me," I say quietly, looking at the floor.

He moves right in front of me. Chris lifts my face to look into my eyes. "Who was the guy?"

"He's just my friend, Graham. He is not interested in me at all, and I'm definitely not interested in him."

Chris nods and then looks around. "Where's Madison?"

"She's at Mom and Dad's. We were going to spend the night there." I shrug. "I just didn't want to be alone tonight."

He cups my face in his hand and I nervously lick my lips. My heart pounds in my chest. "Tell me not to kiss you," Chris whispers.

"No," I whisper back.

"You deserve someone better than me." His voice is rough, and he looks so vulnerable right now.

I cover his lips with my finger. "I deserve who I want. Why can't you see what a good person you a—"

Before I can even finish speaking, he slams his lips down on mine. I wrap my arms around his waist. He uses his lips to open my mouth. Chris swallows my moan the moment his tongue brushes mine.

He wraps my braid around his hand, pulling my head back. I gasp against his lips and grip onto him tighter. He pulls back and his breath leaves him in rapid pants. Chris steps back from me and my heart sinks.

"I'm sorry. I shouldn't have done that."

"What are you talking about? I wanted you to do it, I've wanted you to do it for a long time." I step toward him. "I like you, Chris. Not just because you're Madison's father, but because you're a wonderful dad, a wonderful son. I like you because you're sweet to me, I like talking to you because you really listen to what I have to say."

"You take my breath away," he whispers. "Even in your scrubs after working all day, you're gorgeous. The way you look at our daughter makes me envious because I want you to look at me like that too." A tear slides down my cheek and he continues speaking. "You've had my back since I've been home. You let me know our daughter with no questions asked."

"There was never any question. I never would've kept her from you." I take a step toward him as butterflies take flight in my belly. "I like you, Chris." I reach out with both hands and grab his face.

"You already said that," he says right before I move in and kiss his lips. Chris lets me control the kiss for about two seconds before we're moving and my back hits the wall.

He grabs me by my thighs, lifting me off the ground until my legs are wrapped around his waist. I'm so nervous. I haven't had sex with anyone but him, and it was only the one time.

I can feel he's hard and my body does a shiver. He pulls away from my lips and begins kissing down my cheek, and then dragging his tongue to where my neck meets my shoulder. He nips at the tender skin, making me moan. "Tell me to stop," Chris whispers against my ear.

"I can't," I whimper.

Chris carries me through my apartment, into my

bedroom. My nerves kick in the moment my back hit the mattress. He closes his eyes and then lays his head on my chest. "I don't have any condoms," he says quietly.

"Ohh…" I say, disappointment filling me.

He moves us around so we're lying on our sides, facing each other. Chris surprises me by grabbing my hands and pulling them to his mouth so he can kiss them. "I'm sorry."

"Don't be sorry," I tell him honestly. "I'm sorry I don't have any."

His smile makes him look young and carefree, how I remembered he looked when we were younger. "Can I take you out to dinner tonight?"

I nod. "I'd like that."

Chris moves to get up and grabs my hands, helping me up and out of bed. He tips my head back and kisses me softly on the lips. "How about I come back in an hour to pick you up?"

"That sounds good." I walk him toward the door. "If Mom and Dad can keep Madison all night you could plan on staying here." I've never been bold in my life. I'm surprised with myself.

"Okay, I'd like that, but why don't we pick up Madison after dinner, then I can spend the night with both of you."

I'm not sure why, but that tickles me. I love that he wants our daughter here as well. "Okay, that sounds great.

Chris kisses me one more time. "Be back in an hour." I shut the door behind him and then jump up and down, clapping quietly.

Shoot, now I have to figure out what to wear.

CHRIS

I'm rubbing some styling cream through my hair, trying to wrangle it into submission when there's a knock on my bedroom door. "Come in," I call out. Dad appears in the doorway to the bathroom a moment later. "Hey Dad."

"You look nice, do you have a date?" he says hopefully.

I smile and nod. "Yeah. I'm taking Haddie out for dinner tonight."

His face lights up even more—I know his hope is that she and I become a couple, whether it is for Madison's sake, I don't know, but he talks about how Haddie and I make a good team. I just haven't wanted to get his hopes up.

The truth is, I like her...a lot, and it's not just because she's the mother of my child. She's only twenty, but she's so mature. She believes in me and gives me the strength to feel like I can do anything.

It doesn't hurt that she's fucking stunning, and for someone inexperienced, when she kisses me, I feel it in my soul. Fuck, that sounds cheesy, but it's the truth.

"That's great! Who has the precious girl tonight?" Of course, Dad's beaming, this is what he wanted.

"Journey and Dylan, but we're going to pick her up after we're done. You know, just hang out together." I wash the styling cream off my hands. I turn to look at him and he's smiling wide.

"Well, I'll let you finish getting ready, but please send Haddie my love, and kiss that precious girl for me." He starts to walk away, but he stops and turns back to me. "I'm really proud of you, son. I-I know your mom is looking down on you and she's so proud of you too."

I walk over to him and pull Dad into my arms, giving him a back slapping hug. "Thank you for believing in me and helping me get help, cleaning up my life. I love you."

"I love you, too, son."

He leaves me to finish, and I get dressed in a pair of jeans and a royal blue polo. I slip on a pair of tan Birkenstocks. I pull my gym bag out of the closet and throw a change of clothes into it, and grab the box of condoms I bought.

Earlier I wanted nothing more than to be inside her, and it took all my willpower not to just say fuck it and take the chance of getting her pregnant again, which is so fucking irresponsible.

Thankfully, I was smart and stopped it. I don't know if anything will happen tonight, but I want to be prepared just in case. I throw the bag over my shoulder, and I head into the family room. "Dad, I'm heading out."

He gets up from the recliner. "Son, you aren't a teenager anymore. You don't have to check in with me." Dad chuckles, making me smile. "You kids have fun tonight."

I head out to my truck, tossing the bag into the passenger seat. By the time I pull into the parking lot at Haddie's apartment I'm a ball of nerves. I've never had an issue with women, getting them or fucking them. Back in my partying days I had plenty of girls ready and willing to burn up the sheets with me.

Hell, I've had orgies that would make a porn star blush—I'm not proud of my behavior, because I've treated women like they were basically fuck toys. I know that sounds gross, but it's the truth.

Shit, my daughter was conceived when I was blackout drunk. I hate that, it's not like Madison will ever know, but I will and so will Haddie. My hope is that I can at least erase that memory from Haddie's mind by giving her a better one.

I jog up the stairs and knock on the door. The lock disengages and then the door opens. "Wow." That's all I can say. Haddie is in a red tank dress, with a flowy skirt that hits her mid-thigh—showing off her long legs. She's always been slim, but now her breasts are bigger and she's got a hint of curves.

"I look okay?" Her voice is shaky, she's nervous.

I step toward her so we're almost touching. "You look fucking beautiful."

Her cheeks turn a deep shade of pink. "Thank you. You're looking good yourself." Haddie holds out her hand. "I'll take your bag to my room."

I hand her my bag and follow her inside, shutting the door behind me. She disappears down the hall and I wait in the living room. I smile when I look at the picture of Madison. She's facing the camera, her face resting in her hands, and she's clearly sleeping.

Dad has the same picture hanging on the wall. I hear footsteps a moment later and Haddie comes down the hall. I hold my hand out to her. The moment she places hers in mine, everything feels perfect, we're just missing our baby girl.

We head down the stairs when a door opens. "Hey Haddie." It's her neighbor, Lance. "Hey Chris."

When we reach the bottom I hold my free hand out to him. "Hey Lance, how's it going?"

"Hi, Lance," Haddie says as she gives him a little wave.

"Where's the little one?"

"Grandparents," We tell him at the same time. After saying goodbye, I lead Haddie to my truck, and then we head to dinner.

* * *

TONIGHT DID NOT GO the way that I'd hoped. Dinner went well, hell, better than well.

I took Haddie to the Waterfront and we sat on the patio and were surrounded by twinkle lights. After the waiter came and took our order, I grabbed her hands and held them, and she smiled at me.

"I'm glad we're doing this," she said quietly. "This is my favorite place to eat."

I stroke the back of her hands with my thumbs. "I'm glad we are too. Tell me how work is going. Are you still on the modified orientation?" I haven't seen her in action since she's become a nurse, but I saw the way she took care of my mom.

She's compassionate and a natural caretaker—that's probably why she's such a wonderful mother.

"I am, but I met with my preceptor, and she talked to me about increasing my caseload. I love it though, and I know that's weird because my patients pass away, but I get the privilege to help them pass with dignity." She looked anywhere but at me. "Sorry, that probably sounds lame."

I shook my head and tugged on her hands until she looked at me. "Not at all. There is nothing wrong with loving what you do. Some people aren't lucky enough to get to do what is their passion."

"Thank you for saying that."

Our waiter interrupted us to set our food down. Haddie had me cracking up when she leaned down, smelling her steak. "Does that smell good?" I asked with a laugh.

"Sorry, I'm starving, and they grill the best steak. Just don't tell my dad that." She cut into her meat and moaned as she stuck it in her mouth.

My dick twitches in my pants. "Ahem…" I dig into my scallops. Damn, I missed this place. "I ran into your brother and Chloe the other night."

"Really? Where at?"

I knew she would ask and I'm slightly embarrassed to say it. "I was…uh—leaving a meeting. They were across the street. That little boy looks just like his dad."

Haddie beamed. "He does and he's so wild, but so sweet." She grabbed her phone and then turned it toward me.

I took it from her and smiled. JJ was squatting down next to Madison in her carrier, bending over, and was kissing her head. I love that our kids are close in age, I hope they're close. Maybe one day we'll be back there again. Hell, I would take him treating me as an acquaintance as long as he was in my life.

I handed the phone back to her and we finished our dinner. We held hands on the way to her parents' house to pick up Madison. I'm a little nervous because things are still awkward between Dylan and I, but I'm always going to be around, and we have to be able to coexist for her.

We pulled into the driveway and I got out, coming around to open Haddie's door for, helping her down. With her hand in mine, I led her to the front door. It opened the moment we stepped up onto the porch. JoJo was smiling at us. "Hey guys. Madison is on the floor with her papa."

Stepping side, I held Haddie's hand as we made our way to the family room. Sure enough, Madison was on her belly, squealing and kicking her legs at her papa. He smiled when he saw us, or I should say when he saw Haddie.

He scooped my girl off the floor, and she kicked her legs when she saw us. Surprisingly, Dylan handed her over to me. "Hey, baby girl. I've missed you." I kissed the top of her head.

"How was she?" Haddie asked, wrapping her arms around her dad.

"Perfect as always," JoJo said, smiling at her daughter and granddaughter.

We got Madison strapped into her carrier and I carried her toward the door. "Thank you again for watching her," I told them as they walked us to the door.

Haddie grabbed my hand, lacing our fingers together. I certainly didn't miss the daggers Dylan was shooting at me.

JoJo, on the other hand, kissed my cheek before hugging and kissing her daughter. Once I got Madison loaded in the back, I opened the door for Haddie, helping her inside.

Back at Haddie's, I took care of Madison's diaper and put her in her jammies, while she changed. I'm still awkward when I do both, but every time I get a little bit better. When Haddie came out free of makeup, in a black tank top and red knit shorts, she never looked sexier.

I got off the floor with Madison in my arms, kissing her cheek until she started cooing and laughing. We switched off and I went into the bedroom to change into cut off sweats and an old Foo Fighters t-shirt.

I stood in front of the door, and before I opened it, I took a deep breath and shook out my hands. I was so nervous, more nervous than I've ever been. It's been so long since I've had sex and certainly a long time since I've had sex sober.

What if I disappoint her? I did once before. She was a virgin, and I made her first time, well hell, I don't know how I made her first time because I was blackout drunk and on a coke bender. Hell, I'm surprised I was even able to perform.

"Don't be an idiot," I whispered to myself.

I then made my way back out to my girls.

It was two hours later that our night took a turn. After I put Madison to bed, I came back out to the living room and sat on the sofa, wrapping my arm around Haddie's shoulder, and we went back to watching our movie.

I felt it, the moment she fell asleep with her head on my chest. I wrapped my arms around her, and kissed the top of her head.

I woke with a start as did Haddie, then we realized that Madison was screaming bloody murder. We ran into the nursery—my sweet daughter had shit up her back and up her front, and was beet red. Ignoring the smell and the fact it was about to get all over me, I picked my baby girl up and immediately panicked. "She's burning up."

Of course, Haddie the nurse was cool, calm, and collected. She grabbed the thermometer and touched it Madison's forehead. When it beeped she pulled it away. "It's 100.1. I'm going to get the Tylenol." She disappeared out of the bedroom.

That brings us to now. "Shh...baby girl. It's okay," I croon. My heart is breaking because she sounds miserable.

Haddie comes back in with an eye dropper full of red liquid. She grabs Madison's face and squirts the medicine into her mouth. The baby makes a god-awful gurgling, coughing sound, and then she starts screaming again.

"Let's get her cleaned up," I say, and we head into the bathroom in Haddie's room. She gets the shower going and then takes Madison, while I quickly strip down to my boxer briefs. Haddie hands me the baby and I strip her down, and then climb into the shower, getting my baby girl clean.

HADDIE

here is nothing sexier than a man taking care of his child. When I come back from throwing the bedding and their clothes in the washer, I watch as Chris rinses Madison's little body off even as she screams her head off. I soap up a washcloth and reach in, running it over her body and Chris's.

Once they're cleaned off, Chris hands me the baby and I wrap a towel around her. He steps out and I try to ignore the fact that his body is so sexy; it is muscular, but not overly so. Chris has almost an eight pack, and that V that I've read about in my romance stories. I won't lie, he looks better than ever.

By the time Madison is in clean jammies her cries are no longer pained. We lie on my sofa, he's on his back with our daughter on his chest and I've got my back against the cushions. Our legs are tangled together as we both watch her back go up and down as she starts to fall asleep.

We're up and down all night until Madison's fever finally breaks.

I carry two cups of coffee into my bedroom and find

Chris shirtless and laying on his side, with his hand resting on our sleeping daughter's chest. He sits up and takes the mug from me.

"I didn't know how you take it, so it's black." I sit down by his legs.

He smiles at me and gosh, he is sexy. His hair is messy, and his eyes are soft with sleep. It doesn't hurt that he's not wearing a shirt. God, I want to bite each of his muscles. "Baby, if you keep staring at me like that, we're going to have to figure something out."

I get what he's implying, and my cheeks heat up. "How is she?" I ask, wanting to change the subject.

"She's whimpered a couple of times in her sleep, but she didn't wake up." He kisses her forehead and then smiles at me. "I've never seen so much poop come out of a little baby before."

"Well, I'm proud of you. I thought for sure you were going to start gagging."

He shrugs. "I think it helped that I knew she didn't feel well that kept me from really thinking about it." Chris looks down at Madison and then back up at me. "Should we put her in the crib?"

I nod and he stands up. He carefully scoops her up and cradles her in his arms. She squeaks, but then settles against her daddy's chest. I follow him into her bedroom, and he lays her down on her clean bedding. I step up beside him and wrap my arm around his waist. Madison rolls to her side and continues to sleep. He wraps his arm around my shoulders, and we stand beside the crib, watching our baby sleep.

"She's the best thing I've ever done," Chris whispers.

I wrap my other arm around him, hugging him tight. "Same," I whisper, and then lay my head on his shoulder. "We should try and get some sleep, just in case it's she wakes again."

We head into my bedroom and both crawl into bed. Chris pulls me toward him until we're lying chest to chest. I tangle my legs with his. "Thank you for helping with Madison all night."

"There was no place I'd rather be, than right here with you two."

I reach out and stroke his stubbled cheek with my thumb. I lean forward, pressing my lips to his. His kiss is tentative, but I power on and flick my tongue against his lips.

He wraps his arm around me and up into my hair. Chris rolls us so he's on his back and I'm straddling him. Our kiss intensifies and I moan as his tongue tangles with mine. God, he can kiss, and I feel it all the way down to my nether region.

Chris is hard and it feels so good in between my legs. I begin to rock my hips, rubbing against him. He grips my hips and thrusts up against me. He slides his hand under my shirt —I help him pull it off. I'm wearing a nursing cami that's perfect because even breastfeeding, my boobs are still small.

He rolls us so I'm on my back and he's between my legs, his mouth still on mine. Chris pulls his mouth away and begins to kiss down my neck, nipping at my flesh. Goose-bumps pop up all over my body and I moan.

His lips travel down further and when his lips wrap around my nipple, my back arches off the bed. Chris takes his time between both breasts, licking and sucking my nipples. When a little milk comes out, I watch as he laps up the white drops.

It shouldn't turn me on, but it really does. He makes little "mmm…" sounds and I feel it right between my legs.

Chris pushes away from me, taking my shorts with him. "Don't move," he says, his voice husky. He goes to his bag and pulls a box of condoms out, tearing it open when he reaches the bed. He throws one next to my head then crawls back onto the bed.

My hands immediately go to his head at the first swipe of his tongue against my pussy. I bite my lip to keep from crying out as he sucks my clit into his mouth. I have no experience really, except for the one time…with him.

In no time at all I begin to come, pumping my hips toward his mouth. Chris gently brings me down and then he gets up again to strip off his shorts and boxer briefs. I try not to stare at his penis, it's long, thick, and pointing straight up.

He gets between my legs again and grabs the condom, sliding it down his length. Chris bends down, kissing me, reaching between us to rub my clit. I moan against his mouth as he primes me again.

I feel him at my entrance and then he begins to ease into me. "God, you're so tight, baby," he whispers against my lips. "Tell me if I hurt you."

I nod as he works himself in and out of me—the wet sounds my body makes should embarrass me, but I'm too turned on to care. Chris pulls almost all the way out, and then pushes in until he bottoms out.

I start to come and he thrusts into me in powerful strokes as I grab onto my headboard. He leans down, licking the milk that I'm leaking. "You feel so good, I'm going to come so hard."

Chris pushes up and thrusts into me once and then twice before planting himself deep. I feel his cock jerk inside me, causing me to shiver. He collapses on top of me and I wrap my arms and legs around him, nuzzling his neck.

"Sorry that was over so quick," he says quietly. "Next time will be better."

I pull back. "Um…that was amazing. I mean, you're the only person I've ever slept with, but this was amazing."

He pulls out of me and the rolls us so we're chest to chest. "Did I make it good for you...before?"

I hate that he doesn't remember, but he was sick. "You were gentle," I tell him softly. "You made sure I had an orgasm before we had sex. I promise that you were sweet and took your time." Chris closes his eyes. I grab his face and he opens his eyes. "I swear, it was good for me."

"Thank you." Chris leans in and kiss me. "I better get rid of this condom, then we should get some sleep.

I watch him as he walks naked into my bathroom. While he's taking care of business, I throw on my tank top and shorts and am just climbing back into bed when he comes out.

"You're so beautiful, and I know that's weird to say to a guy, but you are." I get up on my knees, watching him blush while he throws his underwear and shorts on. "Oh my gosh, you're blushing."

I squeal as Chris tackles me to the bed. We kiss for a few minutes and then we get settled in to sleep.

CHRIS

*H*addie sleeps beside me and I can't keep my eyes off her. She's beautiful, but when I saw her last night, caring for our daughter, she was stunning. I reach out, fingering a strawberry blonde curl. I wonder if Madison will have the reddish blonde hair as well.

I let go of her hair and Haddie's eyes flutter open. She smiles at me. "Why are you staring at me, weirdo?" She starts to giggle and I grab her, pulling her on top of me.

I reach up, pushing her hair back. "Because you're pretty to look at." I give her what I hope is a cheeky smile. She leans down, laying on my chest. I hug her tight and kiss her temple.

We begin to make out again when a certain someone begins to cry. I roll us over. "Stay here and I'll get baby girl." Haddie nods, and I climb off the bed. I step into Madison's room. "Hey, my sweet girl." She begins to kick her legs and stretch out her arms.

I pick her up and take her over to the changing table. Luckily, her diaper is just wet. I get her all cleaned up and powdered before putting her diaper on. After snapping her jammies back up, I lift her.

Madison snuggles against my chest, and I hug her to me. "Let's go see Mommy."

Haddie sits up when we come in. "Madison," she says in a sing song voice. I crawl on the bed and hand her over to her mom. "Are you hungry?"

I watch as Haddie lies on her side and pulls up her tank top and Madison latches on to her mom's breast. I get situated on my side and my daughter grabs my finger while she nurses.

I look up to see Haddie watching me with a smile on her face. She puckers up when I lean forward to kiss her. "I can't stop kissing you," I whisper against her lips.

"That's good, because I like kissing you," she whispers back.

In my life, I have never felt like this with a woman. It was always the game of how quickly I can get a girl into bed. Who cares what her name is or anything else about her, but with Haddie, I want to know everything about this amazing woman.

"Does it hurt?" I ask as I look down at Madison, latched onto her mommy's boob. "She's sucking pretty hard."

"It doesn't hurt, now when she's got teeth it might, but for now I'm so used to it they're a little toughened up."

Madison releases her mom's nipple and smiles at us, then pulls my finger toward her mouth. "Oh no, sweetheart." I look at Haddie, "uhh…we haven't showered, and you know we kind of—you know."

"Oh yeah." She smiles and her cheeks turn pink.

I sit up, bringing Madison with me and burping her. She burps and then toots, making me laugh, but the moment she lays her head on my chest I melt into a huge puddle. I kiss the top of her head. "It is amazing how she can show me without words that she loves me. I love you so much, baby girl."

"She knows," Haddie says with a smile. "I'm going to make some coffee." She climbs off the bed. Madison and I follow her into the kitchen. While our daughter babbles in her secret baby talk, I lean against the counter and watch Haddie get the coffee going.

"Whatever was wrong with her must have run its course, right?" I place my hand on Madison's forehead. "She's definitely not running a fever."

"It was likely just a bug, but I'll call her pediatrician tomorrow and see if I should bring her in." The coffee beeps and Haddie pours us both a cup. I place Madison in her bouncy seat and grab my cup of coffee.

"What's on your agenda for today?" I lean against the counter, taking a sip of my coffee.

"Relax, relax, and relax some more. Would you care to join us?" Haddie grabs Madison's foot and acts like she's eating it.

Our daughter coos and laughs, making me smile. "I'd love to. How about we order a pizza for dinner?"

"That sounds good. If you keep an eye on her, I'll make us some eggs and toast."

I step to Haddie and grab her hip. "Sure, baby." I lean in, kissing behind her ear. She sighs and it makes me smile. "Now you come with me, baby girl." I pluck her from her bouncy seat and carry her into the living room.

I lie on my back on the sofa while she's on her tummy on my chest. Madison smiles at me and pushes up with her arms. "Oh my god," I whisper as the most heinous, wet fart sound comes from my beautiful little girl. She then starts to cry. "Hey babe, she had a blow out. I'm going to clean her up," I holler and then get off the couch.

In her room I lie her on the changing table. Her cries are

breaking my heart. "I know, sweetheart, Daddy's going to get you all clean." I undo her diaper and hold my breath when I see the funk.

I quickly get her cleaned up and I start softly singing, making up a little song about little girls and unicorns. It's complete nonsense but she stops crying, so I'm calling it a win.

Once she's all snapped back into place, I pick her up and kiss her cheek. "No more blow outs, okay?"

She babbles and then smiles at me. I turn around and find Haddie standing in the doorway watching us. "Is she all clean?"

"Yep, it was pretty bad, but not like last night."

We head out to the kitchen where our eggs and toast are waiting. I grab Madison's bouncy seat and carefully place her in it before washing my hands. While drying them, I sit down at the table, drop the paper towel, and dig in. "These are great."

"Thanks. I'm not the best cook, but I make really good eggs. So...that song was really cute." She smiles cheekily at me and digs into her eggs.

"Thanks. I didn't even know what the hell I was singing. I was just trying not to gag." Haddie laughs and it is music to my ears. "You're so pretty, but you stink." I grab my daughter's foot, shaking it.

"Yes, she does. I've heard it gets worse once she starts eating baby food."

I make the gagging motion, causing her to laugh. God, I love that sound.

We finish breakfast, spending the rest of the day snuggling with our girl, and when she's sleeping, we make out like a couple of teenagers. If we could spend every day like this I'd be a happy man, but then there is that little voice in my head, telling me I should step back, that I'm not ready for all of this—that I'm going to screw it up and lose them both.

I just hope that it's not true.

* * *

I STEP into the coffee shop and spot Mark over by the window. After ordering a coffee and a chocolate croissant, I stand over by the counter waiting to pick it up. Once I have both in hand I walk over to his table.

"Hey man," I say as I reach the table. I set my stuff down and he stands up so we can exchange a bro-hug. Mark and I went to school together, but he was a grade higher. We ran into each other at an AA meeting and we stood outside having a cigarette. He's been sober for five years and agreed to be my sponsor.

"Good, bro. How are things?" He takes a drink of his coffee.

I nod. "They're great. Work's been good, the rest of the crew is finally starting to warm up to me. Dylan no longer looks like he wants to murder me."

Mark starts laughing, too bad it's totally true.

It's been two weeks since the first night sleeping over at Haddie's, and honestly things are great. Dad still watches Madison two days a week and on those days, Haddie comes over and makes dinner, and the three of us eat together.

The two days JoJo has her, I have started picking her up and taking her back to Haddie's apartment and have been spending the night. I've become insatiable for her. What she lacks in experience, Haddie makes up for in enthusiasm.

She's becoming a wild cat and I've enjoyed every single second of it.

"Well, that's good." He shakes his head. "Have you and Joe talked?" Mark knew Joe as well.

I sigh. "No, that's the one thing that sucks. I just have no idea how to heal that breach."

"I wish I had the answer. Maybe ask him to meet you for lunch or something. Lay it all out for him, and if he still can't forgive you, then that's on him. He's mad because of Haddie, right?" I nod. "She's not mad at you, and honestly, she's the only person you should be worried about. I know you and Joe used to be super close, and it sucks, but you may never get that back." He's quiet for a minute. "You know my story. I fucked up and I have to live with that forever."

He got married right before he started law school. Mark began to drink heavily and ended up getting kicked out of school—he hit rock bottom when he cheated on his wife, who was pregnant with their son, and she didn't even give him any chances, just packed up and left.

Mark ended up with a DUI. He got help, and now he's able to co-parent with his ex and her new husband. He hates that he hurt her because of his drinking, but he's learned to live with it.

"This is all so much harder than I ever thought it could be."

"Of course it is, you hurt him. If he forgives you and you can gain back his friendship, then that's great. You just have to be prepared for it to go either way." Mark takes a drink. "How is your dad doing?"

I smile. "He's doing great, or at least as good as someone can be after their wife passes away. While I was in California, Haddie was there for him and she included him in a lot of prebaby stuff. I think it gave him purpose. Hell, he was there when Madison was born."

"That's great. That was your mom's name, right?" I nod. "Let me see her picture."

I grab my phone and unlock it before pulling up my

photo app. I open the newest folder I made and hand it to him.

He smiles as he looks them over and then turns my phone toward me. It's the picture that is also my screensaver. Haddie is curled up next to me and I'm holding Madison in my arms. "This is a really sweet picture. Good thing she looks like her momma."

"I know right, she's beautiful."

We get up and head outside. "Will I see you at the meeting tomorrow?" Mark asks. I stop right outside the door.

"Yeah, I'll be there." I slap him on the shoulder. "I'll see you later."

I reach my truck and head toward Haddie's, ready to spend time with my girls.

HADDIE

"$\mathcal{M}$rs. Meyers, this is the number to the office. If you need anything at all, don't hesitate to call. I'll get Carl's prescriptions called in for you. Home Care Products will contact you about the hospital bed." I hand my new patient's wife the magnet with our number on it.

"Thank you, Haddie," one of his daughters says.

I stick my laptop into my backpack and take my leave. Once I'm back at the office, I finish my charting, putting my orders in, and getting his medication called in. My phone beeps beside me. I pick it up and smile because it's a text from Chris.

Chris: Hey, I got done early today, look who decided to join me for an afternoon snooze.

The picture he sent is him lying on his back with Madison asleep on his chest. My heart melts and I save the photo and make it my screensaver. I'm falling in love with him and I don't know what to do about it.

I know he's been through a lot over the past year and I don't want to add any unnecessary stress. In other words, I'll keep those feelings buried deep because I'm not sure he feels the same way. My only hope is that I won't have to watch him walk away and proclaim his love to someone else.

My phone vibrates again and I see he sent me another text.

Chris: Madison told me that she'd like you home soon because we miss you. *He also* included a heart emoji.

He is making it really hard to push those feelings down.

Haddie: Well, I miss you guys too. I have one more patient to see and then I'll be there.

I get back to work, but I do it with a smile on my face.

* * *

I CRAWL up Chris's body, grabbing his cock in my hand before lining him up and sinking down on him. Both of us moan as he grabs my hips and begins rocking me. In no time at all I've become a horny monster who thinks about sex constantly.

My head falls back, and I moan as he hits deep inside me. He pushes up and wraps his lips around my nipple. I wrap my arms around his head as I cry out. "Oh god, yes!"

Chris tips his head back and I attack his mouth as he grabs my hips, fucking me up and down on him. His tongue duels with mine and I moan into his mouth. On every downward thrust I feel him hit my clit.

My orgasm begins to build and I begin to rock harder on top of him. He reaches in between us and begins to rub my clit. My body winds up for a huge explosion as I whimper into his mouth.

He pulls his mouth away and whispers against my lips. "Are you going to come for me?"

Chris grips my hip with his free hand and then begins kissing my neck. The moment he nips at my flesh, I detonate. He covers my mouth as I ride my orgasm out.

He flips us and begins thrusting into me with abandon. Chris clenches his eyelids shut and begins to fuck me erratically until finally he comes, groaning into my neck. I wrap my arms and legs around him, hugging him tight.

We both pant and I swear my heart is still pounding in my chest. He makes me feel sexy and desirable, something I've never had before. Chris kisses up my neck and then my lips.

He slips his softening cock out of me. "Let me go take care of this. I'll be right back."

I watch him walk in all his naked glory into the bathroom. Chris returns a minute later. "Stop staring at me like that. I need a nap." It's four in the morning and I'd woken up with his hand down the front of my panties. Madison will be up in the next hour so we should go back to sleep.

"Sorry, you're hot," I tell him.

He crawls back into bed and pulls me into his arms. "You're pretty hot yourself." Chris kisses my forehead and then we fall asleep.

* * *

CHRIS IS WORKING late tonight so I'm picking up Madison from my parents' house. When I pull down their street, I spot my brother's SUV in the driveway. I sigh. I wish he'd talk to Chris. He's reached out to Joe a few times to see if he'd be willing to talk, but my brother has refused.

I know it's immature, but I've refused to talk to Joe because I'm so ticked—he should let Chris say what he has to say.

I pull my car into the driveway. Once I reach the door, I knock before walking in. Joe comes walking out of the kitchen in his uniform, and Madison is in his arms.

"Hey," I say and walk toward him, reaching for my daughter. "Hi, baby girl." I kiss her cheek as she babbles and coos. "What are you doing here?" I finally look up at my brother.

"I was in the neighborhood and going on break, so thought I'd stop by and check on Mom. I was glad to see this cutie pie. I'm glad you're here, I've been wanting to talk to you." Here we go. I knew eventually he'd want to do this.

Mom comes up from the basement with laundry. "Hey, sweetheart." I lean down and kiss her cheek.

"Mom, can you keep an eye on Madison while I talk to Haddie?"

"Is everything okay?" she asks as I hand Madison to her.

Joe nods. "Yeah, Mom. We're fine."

He leads me outside and we take a seat on the deck steps. "Okay, let's hear it."

Joe gives a frustrated sigh. "Haddie, what are you doing?"

I turn to look at him. He looks so much like Dad, it's scary. "What are you talking about?"

"Don't play dumb. I've seen you around with him and I know he's been at your place all night."

I close my eyes and count backwards from ten. He's a cop and probably would not appreciate me punching him in the face. "Okay, first of all, don't ever imply that I'm dumb. Also, it is none of your business who is in my home." I cross my arms over my chest.

"Chris is bad news, he shouldn't be anywh—"

I hold up my hand to stop him from talking. "He's changed. You should see him with Madison. He's good with her, he loves her, and she loves him. Hell, I'm falling in love with him. If you'd at least hear him out, you might be able to see that and maybe even forgive him."

"Why would I? He had sex with my baby sister, doesn't remember it, and got her pregnant." He shakes his head. "You're not in love with him. You're only twenty years old, you don't know how you feel."

I stand up and turn around to face him. "Are you kidding me right now? Don't even act like you're Mr. Family Man and know everything about love. Before Chloe you were out banging anything with a pulse. She gave you a chance to prove you were no longer that guy. Why doesn't Chris get that same chance? I forgave him."

"I wasn't drinking like a fish and doing coke like him."

I throw my hands up. "He was sick. Chris got treatment and has been sober for over a year. You should be congratulating him, not ignoring him. What does that say about you, that you can't even hear him out?"

Joe is quiet for a minute and then goes in for the kill shot. "Are you stupid? Goddamn, he'll hurt you and he'll hurt Madison. Don't come crying to me when he does."

I bite my lip to keep from crying. "Gee, Joe, when did you become a fucking asshole? How about this, stay away from me and stay away from my daughter." I march past him and into the house.

Dad's home and has Madison in his arms. "Let me take her. We're leaving."

"What's going on?" Dad asks as he hands me my girl.

I get her buckled in when Joe comes back in. "Keep him away from me," I say and pick up my backpack and the baby carrier.

"Someone tell me what the hell is going on?" Dad looks between the two of us.

I shake my head and point at Joe. "Ask your son."

Outside I get Madison loaded up when my mom comes walking out. "Honey, what is going on?"

I shake my head. If I start to talk, I'm going to cry. "I can't." My voice cracks and my eyes burn.

"Are you okay to drive home? I can take you and have Daddy pick me up."

"I'll be safe. Precious cargo and all." I give her my fakest bright smile. "The minute we're home I'll text you."

"Okay, baby." She grabs my face and kisses my cheek. "I'm going inside and kick some ass."

She makes me smile. "Love you."

On the way home I decide to call Robert. "Well, this is a nice surprise. How are you, sweetheart?" I love that he acts like we just didn't see each other yesterday.

"I'm good. I was just talking to Madison and she said she was in desperate need of a grandpa snuggle. Is it okay if we come over?" I bite my lip, hoping he says yes.

"Absolutely. I can't wait to see my girls." We disconnect and we head toward Robert's.

The moment we pull down the street I spot Robert on the walkway. I can't help it and smile. That man certainly loves his granddaughter, and he loves me too. Of course, the minute I pull into the driveway, the back door is open, and Robert begins talking to his granddaughter.

I quickly type out a message to Chris.

Haddie: Hey baby, I'm at your house with Madison.

I know he's working late, but I just want to see him. It sounds stupid, but I just want a hug.

CHRIS

The minute I step inside, Haddie's in front of me. "Hi." She walks right into my open arms. "Please just hold me," she say quietly.

"What happened?" I ask. My heart starts beating wildly in my chest.

My day had started out great, it was with Haddie lips wrapped around my dick—see insatiable—then we snuggled until our little princess woke up very angry. We snuggled with her after she nursed and then reluctantly got up to get ready for work.

Haddie looked hot in her scrubs, all professional. I, of course, was just in a t-shirt, jeans, and my steel-toed boots. We made out a little bit before she left to head to her office.

Then Madison helped me make my lunch. When I dropped her off at Journey and Dylan's, she greeted me with a bright smile. "Good morning, you two." She took the diaper bag from me and I set the carrier on the floor and picked the baby up, giving her a kiss on her cheek.

"Haddie is going to pick her tonight. We're doing the

flooring today, so I'll be working late," I say as I hand Madison over.

"No problem, sweetheart. Have a good day and be safe." I gave her arm a squeeze and then left for the job site.

When I got there Violet and Diego were already there, with her dad, Dustin. I am always the first one to arrive and the last to leave. I'm sure people think I'm being a suck up. Truth of the matter is I like those times when I'm alone.

They were doing a walkthrough and I left them to it. Before he left, Dustin stopped me. "Hey, I just wanted to tell you that your work is really impressive. You're going to help make us a nice profit when we sell this place."

I shook his offered hand. "I appreciate it. Hell, by the time we're finished I may be in the market for a new home." The more I've worked on it, the more I've started falling in love with this place. This is the type of home I'd love to raise my daughter in. I could almost see Haddie sitting on the back steps watching our daughter run around the backyard, maybe with a brother or sister.

I couldn't believe that thought popped into my head, and I didn't freak out. It was the truth though; I'm falling in love with her, and I'm scared. If I fall off the wagon, not only would I hurt Haddie, but I'd hurt our daughter as well.

I was getting everything ready to start the floors when the rest of the crew started showing up, including Dylan, who isn't as hands on as he was before, but he still has no problem getting his hands dirty.

He gave me a chin lift before heading outside to go over more plans with Violet and Dustin. The rest of the workday went good, and we got the flooring done. Tomorrow we'll begin laying the plank flooring and I'm sure I'll be even more tempted to buy it.

Now I focus back on my girl, who seems troubled. She

grabs my hand, dragging me to my room. Once the door shuts, she starts pacing. "My brother is a dick."

"What happened?" I sit on the side of the bed. I won't lie that I'm a little worried about what she wants to say.

"I went to Mom's to pick up Madison and Joe was there." Fuck, this isn't good. "He wanted to go outside and talk."

Haddie immediately begins to cry. "He was such a dick and how dare he hold onto his anger when I forgave you for what happened. That should be enough." She gets down on her knees in front of me. "I told him that you're a good man, a good father, and I'm falling in love with you." She begins to cry harder.

"If I were a better man, I'd tell you to walk away from me, but I can't because I'm falling in love with you too." I tip her head back, attacking her mouth, and biting her lower lip. "You know how it feels to know that someone I hurt, the way I hurt you, could have my back? It feels really fucking good."

"I'm sorry Joe's a dick."

I shake my head. "No, he's not a dick. You're his baby sister. I took your virginity and I was loaded and don't remember doing it. He has every right to be mad. Joe may never forgive me and I have to be willing to accept that." I lean down, kissing her softly on the lips. "Why don't you head back out there? I'm going to take a shower. I stink."

Haddie leans forward and sniffs. She then mimes throwing up, making me laugh. I grab her, tickling her sides until she squeals.

I kiss her and then guide her toward the door. "Now, get." She jumps and squeaks when I slap her on the ass. Once she clears the door I shut it behind her. I can hear her laugh through the door.

That sound makes me smile, that's just what I wanted. As I walk toward the bathroom a heaviness settles in my gut. What if I mess this up beyond repair?

"Fuck," I whisper.

* * *

HADDIE'S WORKING THIS WEEKEND, so baby girl and I are going to do some bonding. It's been almost a month since I told her that I'm falling in love with her. I mean it with every fiber of my being. That little voice in my head tries to pop every now and then, but I fight like hell to push it down.

I hate that Haddie still hasn't talked to her brother. He's tried to reach out several times and she hasn't responded to him at all. I've tried to bring it up, but she changes the subject. Dad says to let her take the time she needs, that they'll eventually patch things up. I just hope it's sooner rather than later.

Madison has changed so much in the past month. She's almost six months old and is already starting to sit up on her own. She says Dada, but of course Haddie says that's not what she's saying, but I say she's just jealous. Her hair is getting thicker and if we're outside, I can see a hint of strawberry blonde and I'm grateful. I want her to be beautiful like her momma.

While she rolls around on the floor, pausing to try and pull her legs into her mouth, I am looking at the pictures of the house we just finished flipping. I've spoken to Violet and Diego, and once the landscaping is finished, they're going to have the house appraised, and then I told them I'd be willing to put an offer on it.

I made Violet promise to keep it quiet until I was ready, but honestly, it is perfect. I hope that when it's ready I can ask Haddie to move in with me. It feels quick, but Haddie's parents got together fast, and the only reason mine didn't was because Dad wanted to be done with law school first.

I grab the backpack thingy to strap Madison to my chest,

and it takes a few tries to get it on right. Madison watches me from her blanket on the floor and I smile. "Are you Daddy's girl?"

"Da, da, da, da," she says with a smile.

"You better start saying Momma soon, baby girl. We don't want her getting jealous, do we?" I ask and she gives me a sweet smile. She's got one little tooth that just popped through. It is so adorable, except now she's a little drool monster. "Should we go for a walk?" She kicks her legs and waves her arms.

I put the backpack on and then I pick her up. It takes me a minute to get Madison strapped in securely. I stand in front of the mirror and take it all in. I'm in basketball shorts, a t-shirt, tennis shoes, and a backward baseball hat—my baby girl is strapped to my chest, and I realize something else. I'm just fucking happy.

With a few taps of my phone, I hold it up and take a picture. I send the picture to Haddie.

Chris: *We miss you and hope you're having a good day.*

I slip my sunglasses on and we head out. While we walk, I make sure I adjust Madison's hat and then turn on one of the sports podcasts I listen to. We walk toward the waterfront, and I smile as she kicks her little legs. Thankfully it's not too hot out. We walk along the path and I notice that baby girl loves to take everything in.

A guy walks by with a cigarette and my mouth waters. I quit smoking a couple of weeks ago because I don't want that shit around my daughter, and cancer is obviously hereditary. It wasn't really hard because I'd already cut down quite a bit, but every now and then I want one.

We stop at a bench and I pull her out of the little carrier and kiss her cheek. "Hey, pretty girl," I say and stand her up on my legs. She smiles at me, and just like every other time I'm filled with nothing but joy.

A breeze runs over us and goosebumps pop up all over my skin. Madison leans toward me, like she's hugging me. "Aww...sweet girl. I love you so much." I close my eyes and savor this moment as I hug her tightly.

I open my eyes and freeze. Abby and her man, Ben, are standing there. I stand up and walk toward them. "Hey guys." I shake Ben's hand and lean down and kiss Abby's cheek.

"Hi, Chris. Please hand me that baby." She opens and closes her hands in a fast motion.

"Man, you better do it before she rips her right from your arms," Ben says, smiling down at her.

I hand Madison to Abby and she snuggles her close. "She's getting so big," she says before kissing the top of her head. "How are you, Chris? You look great."

"I'm good, thanks." I look around me. "Where are the kiddos?" They've got four gorgeous kids.

"They're with my sister today. Dylan showed me the pictures of the house you guys are flipping. It's sick."

I can't help but feel a bit of pride. "I'm actually considering putting in an offer myself. Don't say anything to Haddie, I want to surprise her."

"We won't say anything. Is she working today?" Abby asks, lifting Madison into the air, smiling up at her.

"Yeah, she said she'd be done around two. Little miss and I thought some fresh air would be good."

Abby smiles at me. "Well, I never thought I'd see the day that you'd be wearing a baby." I take Madison and she helps me get her little legs through the holes. "It's a great look."

They head in the opposite direction of Madison and me. The closer we get to the apartment I can feel that she's asleep. Once we get back, Lance, Haddie's downstairs neighbor steps out of his place. "What's up?" I say and stop at the bottom of the steps.

I appreciate the guy standing back since he's smoking.

"Nothing, just taking a smoke break." He looks down at Madison. "She's knocked out." He flicks his ash. "I'll let you get her upstairs. Tell Haddie I said hey."

"Sure, take it easy." I head upstairs and use the key Haddie gave me. Once inside, I head right to Madison's room. I carefully lift her out and lay her down in the crib. She immediately rolls to her side.

I take off the backpack and the carrier. She's got a rocking chair in the corner, so I drag it over to the crib and sit down. I watch the steady rise and fall of her chest and am thrust back to the day she was born.

I keep looking at my phone, last I heard was that Haddie's water broke and her contractions were three minutes apart. I'm going to be a dad; I'm going to be someone's father. That thought has me rushing to the toilet, emptying the contents of my stomach.

I flush the toilet and grab a washcloth, getting it wet and then wiping my face. I brace myself on the sink and look at myself in the mirror. I'm beginning to look like the guy I used to be before I started abusing everything.

During treatment I began doing yoga, and then began running every day on the beach. Paired with eating healthy, it didn't take long before I'd lost the swollen look and the gut. My eyes are no longer bloodshot and I've got a major farmer tan from working outside.

"Hey, you okay?" Nathan, my roommate says from the bathroom doorway.

I take a deep breath and turn to look at him. "Haddie's in labor. Last I heard, her water broke and she's having contractions every three minutes. It's just weird to think that soon I'll be a dad." I look at my feet and shake my head. "I helped create a life and I don't remember doing it. I'm a piece of shit."

"Chris, I OD'd and my kid found me. We've made mistakes and have done things that we can't take back. I know Jonah will be in therapy a long time because of what he saw, but he's a strong kid,

and together we'll work on our father/son relationship and healing the damage I caused. Your son or daughter won't know what you did, and from what I've gathered, Haddie isn't the type of girl who's going to throw that in your face." He grabs my shoulder, shaking it. *"One day at a time."*

My phone peeps and I see it is a text from Dad.

Dad: Haddie's getting ready to push! The baby is coming.

I smile even through the nausea is present. My dad has been looking forward to this since the day he learned he was going to be a grandpa. It just tells me what kind of woman Haddie is—she's let Dad be involved in her whole pregnancy. He'll get to see my child being born.

I thought about flying home, but her family hates me, and I didn't want to cause any unnecessary stress to anyone. So instead, I'll be sitting here waiting to hear the news.

"One day at a time," I repeat his words. "I feel like I should go home." The closer Haddie got to her due date I began to think about going home, beginning to make amends with everyone I've hurt. "I want to have a relationship with my kid, but I can't thank you enough for everything. The job, the place to stay, and your friendship."

We share a bro hug and head out to the living room where I stare at my phone, waiting to hear about the arrival of the baby.

My phone pings an hour later and it's a video from Dad. A screaming baby appears and I hear Dad's excited voice. "It's a girl, Madison Anne." Out of nowhere tears begin to stream down my face. Dad's face appears on the video and he's got tears too and his smile is so damn big. "She's beautiful, son. Seven pounds and two ounces, and twenty inches long. Haddie did so great." The phone moves again and Abby, her big sister appears on the screen and then she points it back to the baby. "Meet your daughter, Chris. She's absolutely perfect and we hope you come meet her in person soon." Dad pops back up. "I hope you'll come home, but not until you're ready. I love you so much and I'll keep an eye on our little angel, Madison." The video ends and the screen goes to black.

The phone falls to the ground as I cover my face. The fact that Haddie named our daughter after my mom means so fucking much to me. Once I get control of myself I pick up my phone and watch the video over and over.

HADDIE

I let myself inside my apartment and find the living room empty. Madison could be napping, so I don't call out. I just head down the hall to her nursery. I smile at the sight in front of me. Our daughter is passed out in her crib and Chris is asleep in the rocking chair.

Abby texted me earlier to tell me that she and Ben had run into Chris and Madison on a walk. She'd sent me an adorable picture of Chris with our girl in a carrier on his chest. They both looked so cute, my heart melted—it is now my screensaver.

I don't want to wake them, so I head back out to the living room. I grab my backpack and set it on the couch. In the kitchen I grab myself a glass of lemonade and carry it back out to the living room.

Once I grab my laptop out of my bag, I pull out my notebook and get busy charting the information from my visits today. I love what I do so much already. I'm not so naïve to think I will always love it, but for now I'm going to enjoy every second.

I am almost done with my second chart when I hear footsteps. Chris comes walking into the living room with Madison snuggled to his chest. He is so hot, but when he's holding our daughter, he's so beautiful it makes my heart hurt. They both have soft sleepy faces. "Hey." I stand up and walk toward them.

"Why didn't you wake me?" he asks as he hands her to me. I push up on my toes and give him a kiss on the lips.

"You were sleeping so peacefully I didn't have the heart to wake you." I sit back down and cross my legs criss-cross applesauce. Madison grabs at my t-shirt and I smile down at her. I swear that once my nipple is out, she's latched onto it. Chris sits down next to me and rubs his hand over her head. "Did you guys have a good day?"

He wraps his arm around my shoulders. "Yeah. We went for a walk and she fell asleep on our way back here. She was kicking her legs the whole way to the path on the riverfront. How was your day?"

"It was good. I only saw four patients today and I'm almost done charting on the second patient." Madison releases my nipple and I switch sides. "What sounds good for dinner?" I ask as I lay my head down on his shoulder.

"Why don't I take my girls out? We can go somewhere family friendly," he says with his lips pressed to my forehead.

"That sounds good." Once Madison is done nursing, I spend a few minutes getting snuggles with her.

Chris takes her from me. "I'll take her so you can finish." They disappear into my room, and I hear the TV click on. I turn back to my computer and get back to charting.

* * *

CHRIS HAS a hold of my hand and in his other is the carrier with our daughter chattering happily to herself. The host of Tacobar holds the door open as we reach the door. We step inside and for some reason feel nervous. I don't know, maybe since this is our first *real* outing as a family.

I even took the time to try and look good. I let my natural waves hang down around my shoulders. I'm wearing a tank top maxi dress the color of raspberries, and a pair of black flip-flops. I didn't bother with makeup except for a little gloss.

Chris looks hot in his khaki shorts and short sleeved button up shirt. He's got a pair of black chucks on his feet. His tan muscles are on display, making my mouth water. We're led to a table with a contraption for us to set Madison's carrier.

I love that he keeps her by him. Our waiter comes and we both order raspberry lemonades. He sets chips and salsa down on the table and then leaves us. "How close are you to finishing the house? I know you said you didn't have much left."

Violet told me that Chris is super talented and they're wanting him to continue helping them flip houses.

"The inside just needs to be wiped down and this week they're wrapping up the outside. Diego already showed me the next house. It's gonna be a lot of work, but this is my first project with them from the beginning. I'm excited about it." He takes a drink. "It feels good to know I'm actually good at things."

The waiter interrupts us and takes our order, and then walks away. "You are good at a lot of things." I know I'm snapping at him, but I don't like the way he said that. "You're a great son, an amazing father, and a good boyfr—um, you know, whatever we are."

Chris grabs my hands. "Am I your boyfriend?"

I shrug. "I don't know. Um...do you want to be my boyfriend?" I giggle nervously.

"Absolutely I do, baby."

I know I'm smiling like a lunatic, but I don't care. I'm so fucking happy right now. Madison squeaks and that has us both turning and looking at her. She smiles and flaps her clutched hands.

"Chris Anderson? Oh my god." A blonde with huge boobs in a tiny black dress runs up to the table. "It is you." She wraps her arms around him, practically shoving her boobs in his face.

It takes him a second to register what is happening and then gently pushes her away. "Hey, Lyla. How are you?" He seems really uncomfortable.

"Oh, I'm so great. I...Oh, whose baby is that?" She waves her red nails at our daughter.

"She's ours. This is my girlfriend, Haddie Carmichael. She's Joe's sister." The woman barely spares me a glance.

Thankfully our waiter comes with our food and finally that terrible woman walks away. "Wow," I say as I shake my head. "You had a thing with her, didn't you?" I take a deep breath. "Sorry, I don't have the right to ask."

He grabs my hands. "You do have the right, and unfortunately, I have slept with her. I wish I could say I was innocent, but I wasn't."

I shake my head. "You don't owe me an explanation. This is a small town...sort of, and it's bound to happen. Chloe still deals with it with Joe. Hell, my dad and uncles all still deal with it."

We dig into our tacos, he got the chicken and I got the smoked brisket. He hands me one of his tacos and I give him one of mine. The tacos are so good, I'm inhaling every single bite. "I'm sorry, but these are so freaking good."

"They're the best I've ever had." He looks at Madison. "Sorry, baby girl, but you're missing out."

Our daughter smiles up at her daddy and my heart melts the way it always does. "Da, da, bah."

I love hearing her say "da" but I am jealous that she hasn't said "ma" yet. I know da is easier, but I'm the one who carried her, shouldn't ma be her first word?

"I love when she says it," Chris says, smiling down at her. He turns and smiles at me. How can I be jealous when he is so happy? "She'll say Mama soon, I know it."

Once we're finished, we head toward the front and I don't miss the girl from earlier staring at us and then types something on her phone. My stomach turns a bit and I wonder how much this is going to happen.

Also what if his old crowd tries to pull back into that lifestyle?

"Haddie." Chris is looking at me with concern all over his face. "Hey, you okay?"

Shit, I school my features. "Yeah, I'm okay. Sorry, I just spaced out." I smile up at him. He grabs my hand and pulls me to him, kissing me softly on the lips.

We head outside and make our way back to the apartment. As soon as we pull into the parking lot, we both stiffen up because Joe is sitting at the top of the stairs. "Shit, why is he here?" I say quietly.

"Maybe this is good thing." Chris grabs my hand. "Come on. You've got this."

I climb out and then meet him in front of the truck. Again, he grabs my hand and carries our daughter with the other. I want Joe to see us together, united. He stands as we get close and smiles at Madison, grabbing her foot and giving it a little shake.

Joe doesn't look at me, but he does look at Chris. "Can we talk a bit?"

Chris has a hopeful twinkle in his eyes, but it makes me nervous for him. I have no clue what my brother is going to say and I can't read him.

"Yeah, sure. Let me just help get Madison settled and I'll

come out." Chris grabs the key I gave him and opens the door for us. He sets the carrier down and gets her out of it, kissing her cheek before handing her to me. "I'll be back soon."

Joe's standing in the doorway, but I don't care. I push up on my toes and kiss Chris softly on the lips. "We'll be here waiting."

They disappear outside, the door shutting softly behind them. "I hope this is a good talk," I say to my daughter, snuggling her close.

Ten minutes have gone by and he hasn't come back in yet, but I haven't heard any fighting. In that time, I've changed Madison's diaper and put her in her jammies. Now we're snuggling on the sofa, watching *Trailer Park Boys* on Netflix.

Maybe it's taking so long because they're patching things up and they're catching up on their lives. I smile because that has to be it. Joe is doing the right thing and mending fences. "Your uncle is finally going to stop being a poophead." I stand her up on my thighs and she loves it—she bounces up and down.

I hear a car door slam and then another. My heart beats wildly in my chest as I get up and move to the window. I look outside and see Chris's truck pulling out of the parking lot and Joe is sitting in his SUV, staring at his lap.

My eyes burn, something bad happened, and it caused Chris to leave and for Joe to sit there looking upset. I move to open the front door, but he immediately takes off before I can do anything.

I close the door and go to my cellphone, and as soon as I open it I see I have a text from Chris.

Chris: You deserve someone better than me, someone who isn't an embarrassment. I just want you and Madison to be happy and he's right, you would be happier without me.

I stick Madison in her exersaucer and try to call him, but I get his voicemail. "Chris, why did you leave?" I'm proud that my voice sounds strong, even though I feel like I'm about to lose it. "Whatever Joe said to you is not true. You are not a freaking embarrassment. You are strong, beautiful, and everything I want." My voice cracks. "Please don't do this to us." I cover my mouth. "Please." I croak before there's a beep.

Madison starts fretting, and I know she can feel the sudden change in my attitude. I quickly dial Robert to get him a heads up. He answers and I begin to cry while I tell him what I am still trying to piece together.

"I'll talk to him and encourage him to reach out to Mark. It's going to be okay, sweetheart, I promise."

We hang up and I pluck Madison out. She begins to fuss and I hug her tightly to my chest. "It's okay, baby. Daddy will come back." Of course, I could be lying to her right now and my heart is breaking.

The rest of the evening I keep checking my phone and all I've gotten was a text from Robert.

Robert: He's here, sweetheart. I'm taking care of him. I'll ask him to call you when we're done talking.

I decide to bring Madison into my room with me. I just don't want to be alone right now. Needing to laugh, I turn on *Friends*. With baby girl at my breast, I snuggle into the pillows. I keep looking at my phone, but it stays silent.

She falls asleep as soon as she's done eating. I make a little wall of pillows so she can't roll off the bed. I know it's not good to have her sleep with me, but I just want her close. I watch the episode where Phoebe teaches, or tries to teach, Joey French. Normally I laugh hard during this episode, but I just don't feel like it.

I watch my hand as it rises and falls as Madison's chest moves up and down. Tomorrow I'm going to get to the bottom of what happened.

It takes a while to fall asleep, but when I do it is such a light sleep.

CHRIS

I stand in the doorway of Haddie's bedroom, watching her and Madison sleep. God, earlier had been a shit show.

As soon as I reached Joe, I crossed my arms over my chest, ready to hear whatever bullshit he was going to spew. He was my best friend, my brother, and I've apologized and tried to make things right, but he won't let me. There was nothing more I could do.

"Why are you here?" I ask.

Joe shrugged. "How am I supposed to believe you've changed?

"You either believe me or you don't. Haddie believes I have and that's all that matters to me." Haddie and my dad are the ones who have believed in me the most, giving me the courage to keep fighting for my sobriety.

"Don't you think this is all embarrassing for my sister? Pregnant by someone who was so fucked up that he didn't remember doing it? Someone who is living with his dad."

I shook my head. "Are you fucking serious right now?" I took a deep breath. "You know, I'm sure there have been plenty of children conceived while the parents were drunk as hell that they don't remember it. Also, not like it's your business, but I'm only living with him until I find a place I want to move to, permanently, with both Haddie and Madison." I held up my hands. "But you know what, I've tried and tried to get through to you, but you were obviously looking for a reason, any reason to end our friendship. I'm sorry. I'm in love with your sister, just to let you know, you know, in case you want to ruin that too."

I jumped into my truck and took off. I quickly texted Haddie, regretting every word I typed out, but truth is, I let Joe's words cloud my judgment. What if he was right? What if I fell off the wagon and embarrassed or hurt her and Madison?

I turned my phone off and drove around before heading to Dad's. He must've known something was up because he was up and coming toward me the moment I stepped inside. "Son, what happened? Haddie called me and she's worried sick."

He made some coffee and then while we sat at the breakfast bar, I told him about Joe's visit, running into a girl I used to fuck, and the uneasy feeling I constantly had in my gut. "Can't you see? Maybe they're better off…"

Dad got out of his chair and grabbed my shoulders roughly. "Son, I love you, but don't fucking finish that sentence." I froze because he's never talked to me like that. "Do you not notice the way that Haddie looks at you? Hell, even your daughter, the minute she hears your voice she searches you out. Are you telling me that you want Haddie to find someone else, someone different, to raise your daughter?" I shook my head.

The idea of my daughter calling someone else Dad killed me. "What if I use again?"

"What if you do? Furthermore, what if you don't? I'm no

expert and have no idea the struggles you're facing every day, but you also have to live your life, otherwise it's going to pass you by." He looked at the floor and then back up at me. "Do you love her?"

I nodded, because it didn't take long for it to happen. "More than anything, but I'm scared I'll hurt them both."

"I get it, I do, but you have to work past that." Dad handed me my phone. "Call Mark, talk to him."

He would be the perfect person to talk to. Mark has been dating a woman since last year and I know in meetings he's talked about his fear of hurting her the way he hurt his ex-wife, and wasn't there for his son at first, but he works hard to be the man he is. From what he says, his woman loves him and his boy.

I did as Dad asked and sat out on the back deck talking to Mark. He let me voice my fears and just listened. When I stopped, he was silent, and then he cleared his throat. "Man, just stop. I know it's scary, but Haddie has a good head on her shoulders. I may not know her, but everything you've said just proves that she's the type of woman you want to have in your corner. Just talk to her, because if you can't do that then you're going to constantly be doubting yourself."

"You're right. I just want to make her proud and show her how I feel about her." He can't see me, but I shake my head. "I want my daughter to feel loved and never doubt that."

"Then do it," Mark said, getting straight to the point. "You want Haddie to be proud, then give her a reason to. You want to show her how you feel, well then, show her. Your daughter already knows you love her. I've seen the pictures of the two of you and it is clear that baby girl has terrible taste in men, because she always smiles at you."

That made me laugh, and it felt fucking great. "Thanks, man, I appreciate you taking the time to talk to me. I know you have your boy."

"Jase is getting some Steph snuggles, so you're not taking my time. Plus, I'm your sponsor and that's what I'm here for. Now get your ass back to your family."

We hung up and I stared across the yard. I knew I needed to go back. Especially after I heard Haddie's message from earlier. It hurt me to hear the pain she was trying to hide.

Now, I'm watching them from the doorway. Haddie's hand rests lovingly on our daughter's stomach. I'm in basketball shorts, so I simply peel off my t-shirt and kick off my tennis shoes. As soon as I crawl onto the bed, Haddie's eyes pop open.

"I knew you'd come back."

I move the pillows and climb in on Madison's other side, leaning down, kissing her forehead. "I'm sorry I left. I let his words get to me."

Haddie whispers, "I'm going to put her in bed so we can talk." She goes to stand up but I stay her with a hand on her arm.

"I'll take her," I say quietly, and then very carefully lift my baby girl off the bed and carry her into her room. Before I lay her down, I kiss her cheek. "I love you so much, baby girl." I put her down and she rolls to her side.

Back in the bedroom, I crawl into bed, and Haddie rolls toward me until when we're chest to chest. "Please don't ever leave like that again," she says softly.

"I promise I won't, and I'm sorry I did." I lean in, kissing her lips.

I pull her until she's on top of me and our kiss turns heated. Haddie immediately begins rubbing against my hard dick, making me groan into her mouth. She pulls back and shakes her head. "No more talk about this. We can talk tomorrow."

In a flash she's up, whipping her shirt off. Fuck, her tits

may be small, but they're fucking phenomenal. I reach up, cupping them in my hands, and tweaking both nipples.

"Mmm...I love that." She moans and then bites her lower lip. "I love you," Haddie whispers.

I pull her down to me, meeting her halfway, attacking her mouth almost violently. She begins to grind against me, moaning into my mouth. Haddie is so turned on I can feel the heat of her pussy.

I reach down and grab the sides of her panties and rip them from her body. With ease I lift her until she's straddling my face. "W-What are y...ahhh," she cries at the first swipe of my tongue. Her sweetness explodes on my tongue. I stiffen my tongue, fucking her pussy. Her cries are music to my ears and in no time, she's coming hard.

I flip us so she's on her back and I'm between her legs. I kiss her, letting her taste herself on my lips. Haddie's tongue peeks out, licking the seam of my lips until I open to her. Our tongues duel and I feel her reach down to my shorts. Her hand wraps around my cock and I grunt into her mouth.

Thank god she's on birth control now because I need to be inside her. "Take me out, baby." She does as I ask, and as soon as my cock is freed, I'm thrusting inside of her. I stay buried to the hilt. "I love you, too," I whisper back. As scared as I am, I can't deny how I feel.

I want the three of us to be a family, and when the time is right I want to give Madison at least one sibling.

I nip at her lips as I begin to move. Fuck, she's so tight and I try to fight the desire to come. I'm not ready for this to be over yet. Haddie begins moving with me, clutching my ass in her hands. She mewls and begins to fuck herself on me. Her nails dig into my ass, and I won't lie, it turns me on so much that my balls are aching for release.

When she lets go, her mouth opens in a wordless cry. Her pussy tightens around me and I begin thrusting into her at a punishing pace, but she takes every thrust. When I begin to come I plant myself deep inside her.

Haddie hugs me tight and nuzzles my cheek. I kiss her forehead and brush her hair out of her face. I slip my softening cock from her body. She shudders and moans as I do it. I situate us so she's lying half on and half off me. I know I should let her clean up, but there is something about knowing that my cum is between her legs.

"I know you've forgiven me, but I just wanted to tell you again, I promise I will never leave like that again. Even if we fight I promise I won't leave."

She tips her head back and puckers her lips and I'm only happy to oblige. Haddie falls asleep first and it doesn't take long before I join her.

HADDIE

*C*hris pulls into the driveway at my parents' house. I called my mom after we got up this morning to see if we could come over and talk to them. I know they know we're together, but I want them to know just how much we are.

I grab his hand and bring it to my lips, kissing the back of it. He smiles at me before throwing the truck into park. Chris hops out and grabs Madison from the back. He meets me at the front end, and we walk up to house holding hands.

Mom opens the door as we walk up the steps. "Hi guys." She looks down at Madison. "There's GiGi's girl." She kisses my cheek and then pulls Chris down to kiss his. Then of course she takes the carrier from him, disappearing inside.

"She loves to steal our baby," I whisper to Chris, making him chuckle. "I'm not sure if she's worse than your dad though. He has her out before I can even shut the car off."

He wraps his arm around my waist and leads us inside. Dad comes out of kitchen as we step inside. "Hey Daddy." I step into his open arms. He hugs me tight and then kisses me on top of the head.

"Hey Dylan." Chris steps forward and holds out his hand. Luckily, Dad takes it.

"I'm glad you guys are here, I wanted to go over some of the plans for the new house we bought to flip, if you're okay doing that after we eat." Dad seems more comfortable around Chris, which is good.

Chris stands a little taller, I'm sure it means a lot that they're enjoying his work. "Yeah, absolutely. I'm excited to get started."

"Come on, guys," Mom says and she sets Madison in the highchair that has sat many grandbabies.

The guys sit down. and I help my mom carry out the platter of French toast, bacon, and scrambled eggs. I sit down next to Chris, and we all load our plates up. There is no conversation at first, we're all too busy stuffing our faces. My mom is an amazing cook and has always loved to cook for her family.

Abby is the same way, but too bad I'm not the greatest cook. Hopefully with time, I'll get better. "This is delicious, Mom, thank you."

"Ba, boo, da, da." Madison hits her chubby little fists on the table. Dad reaches out and shakes her foot. She begins to fuss and reach for her papa. He's a sucker for his grandbabies and lifts her out and holds her while he eats the rest of his breakfast.

Once we're finished, I help Mom clean up. I'm wiping off the counter when I hear Joe's voice.

"What are you doing here, Chris?"

Oh, I'm done with this. I stomp into the living room. "You and me, outside." My brother may be a lot larger than me but I force him outside. "You all please stay in here." As soon as the door is shut I whirl around on him. "What are you trying to do, Joe? I love him, he's Madison's father, and I will not have you treat him like shit." I shove at his chest. "Don't ever try to embarrass him or make Chris feel bad."

Joe moves across the porch. "He could hurt not only you, but Madison too."

"Do you think I'm stupid?" He shakes his head. "Well, quit acting like I have no sense. People change, you've changed. Why is it so hard to believe that Chris has? I never took you for an asshole, Joe, but that is what you're acting like." I move toward him, standing by the steps.

"I'm an asshole because I want to protect my sister and my niece? Wow, he's got you blinded."

I shove his shoulder once and then twice, but the second time he moves back. I stumble and the next thing I know, my clumsy self is tripping over my own feet and falling down the front steps. My face smacks the cement and I immediately begin bleeding all over the sidewalk.

"Jesus, Haddie, are you okay?" Joe gets down in front of me. His face pales and he shouts, "Dad...Chris."

Chris bursts out the front door and jumps down the stairs, grabbing Joe by the front of his shirt. "Did you hurt her?" he barks in his face.

Dad gets in between them, telling them both to stand down.

"Fuck, baby. We've got to get you to the ER." He turns toward my dad and Joe. "Someone grab her teeth." Chris then whips of his shirt and holds it to my face. "Do you have Madison?"

"Yeah, you take care of Haddie. We've got baby girl," Dylan says as he looks at his daughter. "You're okay."

I can only nod. A second later Joe comes running out of the house with a cup in his hand. "It's milk, it says it's better for the teeth. Give me your keys, I'll drive."

Luckily, Chris doesn't fight him. By the time we get to the hospital my face feels like it's doubled in size. Nausea has been swirling in my belly from all the blood I can taste and smell. Joe pulls up in front of the doors.

"Get her inside and I'll park the truck."

I feel him lift me and I lay my head on his shoulder. Inside I hear Chris talking to someone and then we're moving.

It takes a few hours between an ER visit and emergency dentist visit. My teeth are back in my mouth and held in place by wires. If the root doesn't reattach then I may have to get implants. We stop by the pharmacy, and then Chris takes me home.

He leads me into the apartment and gets me set up in bed. Thankfully I was given good pain meds and I'm half loopy. Chris comes back in, carrying a bag. "Lay back, sweetheart. I'm going to put this ice pack on your face.

Not only did I knock my two front teeth out, but I also broke my nose, scraped up my knees, and the palms of my hands. I've always been clumsy, and this just proves it. I doze with the ice pack on my face and I'm not sure how much time passes before I feel the bed compress.

Chris pulls the ice pack off and winces. "Is it twhat bwad?" My mouth is swollen and numb and I talk like a mush mouth.

"It just looks painful." He brushes my hair back. "Your parents had plans to go out of town tonight to go see Parker in Charleston, so Dad's going to keep Madison for tonight. Abby is going to help him if he needs it. They want you to get some sleep." He leans forward, kissing my forehead. "Joe told me what happened." I close my eyes, my anger rising. "He apologized to me."

"Wha?" I try to sit up, but he makes me lay down.

"No baby, lay down. It's all good, I promise. He feels like shit and blames himself for you getting hurt. He told me he's sorry he's been giving me a rough time." Chris sighs. "Baby, I forgive him, because if the roles were reversed and she were my sister, I'd be upset too. I'm not sure if we'll ever be close like we used to be, but I think this will be good."

I nod and wince because my head hurts.

Chris stands up and moves toward the door. "I'm going to go get your prescriptions, some foods that'll be easy for you to eat, and some ice cream." He stops in the doorway and turns to look at me. "I love you."

Will I ever get tired of hearing him say that? I open my mouth to tell him I love him too, but he shakes his head and points to his mouth. I close my eyes, sinking into the pillows, and promptly pass out.

CHRIS

*H*addie sleeps soundly on the sofa while Madison and I go for a walk. It's been three days since her accident. Her eyes no longer look swollen, but they're ringed by dark purple. She's got a splint over the outside of her nose, splints inside to hold her nasal passage open, and it's still packed with gauze. Her lip is still swollen and has dissolvable stitches on the inside of it.

She'll have to wear the wires in her mouth for at least another week or so. Right now she's on an all soft food diet because she can't really chew anything. Madison kicks her legs, bringing my attention back to my baby girl.

I'm holding her hands and she tries pulling one of my fingers into her mouth. She's cutting another tooth because she's a drool monster and tries to chew on everything. "Baby girl, how about I get you a jogging stroller and then you and I can go running? What do you think?"

"Ba, ba, do, dah," Madison chatters happily. She happily kicks her legs as we walk. We stop at the park, and while she's strapped to my chest, I take her on the swings.

Although we don't swing high it's still enough for her to squeal.

I wish I could see her face right now, but the way she's kicking her arms and legs I know she's having a good time.

It doesn't take long before baby girl hits the wall and passes out. I kiss the back of her head and then get off the swings. We make our way back home, and when we step inside, I find some guy sitting on the sofa with Haddie. They turn when I close the door.

"Hi, twhis is Gwam."

The guy stands up and sticks out his hand. "Hey, I'm Graham, a friend of Haddie's."

I haven't met him, but she told me he was a good friend to her, so I take his hand. "Nice to meet you. Haddie's told me a lot about you."

"Same," he says. "I hadn't heard from this one." He points to her. "What happened?"

I give him the version I got from Joe, which is what happened. He didn't sugarcoat blaming himself—that if he hadn't moved when she tried to shove him she wouldn't have fell.

"Damn girl, you really are clumsy." He shakes his head. "Do you need anything? Either of you?"

I shake my head as I pull a sleeping Madison out of the carrier. Haddie holds her hands out and I hand the baby to her.

Graham doesn't stay long, and when he leaves, I walk him out. "What's the damage?" We stop at the bottom of the steps.

"Her nose is broken. She knocked her two front teeth out, and she has them wired into her mouth until the roots grow and attach to her jaw. Her lip is stitched on the inside and she's pretty scraped up." Shit, that's a mouthful.

"Jesus. I know she said she was clumsy, but this is like next level clumsy. I'm glad they have you."

"I'm glad I have them."

He smiles and gives a nod. "Haddie has my number. I'm serious, if you need anything, give me a call."

"I appreciate it. It was nice meeting you." I slap him on the back and turn around to head upstairs. When I step inside, I smile right away. Haddie is asleep with our little girl on her chest. While they nap, I straighten up the kitchen, and then pour myself the last little bit of coffee.

I haven't been on social media much since I got sober—not really wanting to see my old party buds and old fuck buddies. Before I think better of it, I log onto Facebook. I swipe up over and over as I stare at pictures of families, babies, and pets.

My old buddy, Shane, who was also my coke dealer, has a post pop up. It's a picture of him and some of the guys we partied with. He looks swollen, kind of like I did right before I got sober. I pull up his profile page and unfriend and block him, and then spend the next half hour doing that with old party buds and girls I used to fuck.

Once that's done, I don't know how I feel about it and that scares me. I should be happy that I did this. Don't get me wrong, I am, but every now and then there is this teeny tiny piece in my brain telling me that I could drink or use just a little and it wouldn't hurt anything.

I think I need to go to a meeting today. There's one in the basement at the library later today, I think. What is wrong with me? In the living room I find the girls are still asleep. I decide to lie down just for a minute and close my eyes.

I inhale the white power and rub my finger over the mirror before rubbing it on my gums. The bass is thumping and there are women everywhere. In the back of my mind I know there is somewhere I'm supposed to be, but I can't remember.

I pick up my whiskey and take a sip. The vanilla notes are pleasing to my tongue. A statuesque blonde walks toward me.

When she's close enough, I snag her hand and pull her toward me. She's got huge tits and has them practically hanging out.

After I pick up the little vial I empty some of the white powder onto the tit closest to me. I bend down, snorting it up one nostril and then the other. I lick it up and then kiss her, her tongue flicks against mine. She pulls away and then puts my glass to my lips. I drink all the liquor down and resume kissing her.

I move my hands between her legs and I hear someone calling my name. I open my eyes and there is a beautiful strawberry blonde staring at me and a little girl with blonde curls is on her hip.

"Who are you?" I slur.

The little girl begins to cry, burying her face in the woman's neck.

"Who are we? Who are we?" She has her own tears running down her face.

I ignore their tears, I don't know who they are. I drink some more whiskey down and then lean into the blonde.

"Chris? Why are you doing this?" the woman with the child cries.

"Bitch, I don't know you," I shout. Fuck, she's ruining my buzz.

Out of the corner of my eye I watch her hug the little girl and run off. Fuck them and the little voice in my head telling me to go after them.

"Hey, where did that woman go?" Pete, the doorman comes up to me.

"Who cares, we came to party!" I shout and everyone cheers.

He gets close, his face serious. "Man, that was your wife and daughter."

Then like a fast-playing movie, our life comes flashing through my mind. I take off running after them, but they're already gone. I don't know how I make it home, but I do. I step inside and my dad is there waiting for me. "A-Are they here?"

He stands up and shakes his head. "I'm sorry, son. They're gone."

"No, no, no, no," I moan like a wounded animal. My cry rips up from my chest, burning my throat as it leaves me.

"Cwis, Cwis?"

I fly up in bed, clutching my chest. Haddie is standing next to the bed, looking concerned. My breath saws in and out of my lungs. Suddenly, I'm nauseous. I jump up and run toward the bathroom, sliding on my knees to the toilet. I throw up violently over and over until there is nothing left but bile.

The sink turns off and then there's a cool washcloth being placed on my neck. Haddie doesn't say anything. She flushes the toilet and pulls me into her arms. I begin to cry like a baby, unleashing the fear that I had used again. That I'd used and lost Haddie and Madison.

Haddie strokes my hair and lets me wet her shirt with my tears. "It felt so real," I whisper. "I could feel the burn of the whiskey, the numbing feeling on my gums from the coke."

I know this can happen sometimes, but damn, it felt real, and before she can respond the baby cries from the other room. "Go see to her, I'll be right out," I say as I stand up.

She looks me over closely and then nods. As soon as she disappears into Madison's room, I shut the door. I close the toilet lid and sit down. I scrub my hands down my face and shake my head.

I look up and see the bottle of Haddie's pain medication. Pills were never my problem, booze and coke were my drugs of choice. I grab the orange see-thru bottle, unscrewing the cap slowly enough that she won't be able to hear.

Inside the bottle the white pills tempt me. I'm not sure why…maybe it's the dream and I still can't shake the feeling of being fucked up, and maybe I want to chase that high. I tip the bottle until one pill falls into the palm of my hand.

I hold it between two fingers and look at it, like I'm examining it. "Cwis?" There's a knock on the door and I drop the pill and jump up, knocking the pill bottle into the sink. "Hey, you okay?"

"Yeah, baby, I'll be right out." I scoop up the pills and put them back into the bottle and quickly screw the lid back on. *"What the fuck am I doing?"* I whisper. Once I take a deep breath, I open the door to the bathroom.

Haddie is standing in the hallway with Madison in her arms. "Whas going on?" She sounds worried, and I caused that. Is this going to be our life? Her constantly worrying about whether I'm going to use or not?

I can't do this to them. "Come sit with me." I lead her into the living room and sit down next to her. "This isn't easy to say, but I really think I should go. I know I told you I'd never leave again, but you deserve so much better than me. I'm no good for you."

She shakes her head. "Don't say thwat." I reach out, rub the bruise under her right eye.

"Baby, you got hurt while arguing with your brother about me. All I've done is ruin things since I came into your life. I left you to deal with a pregnancy that wasn't planned, being a single mother while starting your career."

Haddie opens her mouth, but I shake my head. I know she's still sore and it hurts to talk. Madison must sense our tenseness because she starts to fuss. I take her and hug her tight. "Shh…It's okay, sweetheart." I kiss the top of her head and she rubs her forehead against my chest. I love when she does that.

"How cud you fink I'd regwet anything?" she says as she looks between the two of us.

"I almost took one of your pain pills. I had it in my fucking hand and was ready to pop it into my mouth. I knocked the bottle into the sink and that stopped me from taking it."

She grabs my phone from the coffee table. "Call Mawk.

Pwease, don't weave. You can't keep wunning when fings get hawd."

A part of me wants to cry, but damn, a part of me wants to laugh because I know she's being sincere and heartfelt, but she sounds so adorable trying to talk.

Haddie crosses her arms over her chest and I know she knows what I was thinking. It is confirmed when she flips me the middle finger.

I grab her hand. "I'm sorry, baby. You're right and that's why I love you. I'll talk to Mark and I'll go to a meeting." I pull Haddie's hand to my lips and kiss the back of it. "Thank you for supporting me, loving me, and kicking me in the ass when I need it."

She takes Madison back, I grab my phone, and then head outside to call Mark.

HADDIE

I pull up in front of Joe and Chloe's place and park.

It's been two weeks since I got hurt. My teeth are fixed, the splints were removed from my nose yesterday. It's still a little swollen, but not noticeable if you don't know me. The bruising is gone in some spots and an ugly yellow color on others.

I decided, and Chris helped me see, that it was time to make up with Joe. Life's too short and we almost lost him once—I'd never forgive myself if something happened to either of us and we didn't work things out.

Madison is with her daddy and they're visiting Grandpa Robert. I climb out of the car and take a deep breath before walking up to the door. It opens as I step onto the porch where my gorgeous sister-in-law is standing.

We walk right into each other's arms, hugging each other tight. It takes a second to realize that there's a belly pressing into mine. I step back and look down, sure enough, she's got a small baby belly. "OMG, you're having another baby."

"Yep, a little girl." She rubs a hand over it. "We just started telling people. I kept cramping and spotting and we just wanted to make sure she was here to stay."

"Oh wow, I'm so happy for you. I hope she's gorgeous, that'll be Joe's payback for his naughty ways," I tell her and spot Joe standing in the living room.

Chloe throws her head back, laughing. "That's what I told him." She turns to look at him. "Didn't I?"

"Yes, you did, repeatedly." He comes toward us and wraps his arm around her. "Little man is zonked out. Why don't you go get some rest?" She nods and then accepts his kiss.

My brother rubs her belly and kisses her one more time before she disappears down the hall. He turns back to me, and I hate the look of sadness I see in his eyes. I step toward him and hug him around the middle. It takes him barely a second before he's got me in a bear hug. "I am so, so sorry," he says into my hair. Joe squeezes me tight, but careful of my face. "Does he make you happy?" I nod. "He loves that sweet little girl."

"He does, and she loves him. They're so cute together. She's starting to crawl, and they get down on the floor, facing each other. He makes animal sounds, and she does this sweet giggle and then she crawls to him. He begins bench pressing her. It is the cutest thing ever. If you'd take a chance on rebuilding your friendship, this improved version of Chris is pretty amazing."

Joe is quiet for a moment. "How'd you get to be so wise?"

"I love you, big brother."

He kisses the top of my head. "I love you, baby sister."

"Dadda." We turn to find Joe's son, JJ standing in the hallway, rubbing his eyes. He smiles and runs toward us, right to his daddy.

My brother scoops him up and kisses his cheek and blows raspberries into his little clone's neck until he squeals. I reach out, brushing his hair out of his face. "Hey buddy."

He smiles at me and gives me a big ol' smooch.

I don't stay too much longer, but when I leave, I feel better about everything.

* * *

One month later

"Do I really need to be blindfolded?" I ask from the passenger seat of Chris's truck.

His chuckle makes me want to stick my tongue out at him. "Yes, baby. Just hang in there. We're almost to our destination." All week he's been acting cagey, and I've been slightly worried. He's been doing so good since his almost slip up, and I know that's not what's going on but he's up to something but I don't know what.

My leg bounces as we slow to a stop, and he shuts the truck off. "Wait for me," he whispers near my ear, making me squeal and jump. A few seconds later my door is opening. "Let me lift you out. I've learned you are very clumsy."

"Hey. I resent that," I say on a huff. It is sad though, because it's true. My face being messed up last month was definitely a sign of my clumsiness. Luckily, I'm almost completely healed. The wire is still helping hold my teeth in —they're no longer wobbly, but I don't see the oral surgeon for another two weeks. Hopefully I can finally eat more foods. I've basically been on a soft food, liquid diet, and it sucks.

I've lost weight I can't afford to lose. The worst part is my milk has dried up, and Madison is completely bottle fed. I'm not happy about it, but there's nothing I can do about it now.

Chris sets me down and moves us a few feet. I feel him get behind me and he places his hands on my hips. Goosebumps pop up all over my body as I feel him place his lips near my ear. "I've been sitting on this for a while, and I hope you love it."

He reaches up and pulls the blindfold down. "Oh my god," I whisper. I take in the two-story home that's in front of me, with a huge sold sign in the yard. "T-This is the house you were working on, isn't it?"

"It is."

"I can't believe you guys sold it so fast, congratulations." I jump into his arms. "I'm so proud of you guys. Was it a young family who bought it?"

He grabs my hand. "You could say that." Chris leads me up to the teal front door. One night I told him I wanted a house with a teal door. It does make me a little sad that he used it on someone else's home. He uses the key to let us inside. The moment I step inside I'm in awe. The foyer is open and the staircase is on the left and to the right is a living room that's open into the dining room. You can get to the kitchen down the hall when you walk in, or when you go through the living room.

The appliances are all stainless steel and there's a white farmer's sink. The countertop and island are a beautiful granite. I smile up at him. "This is really gorgeous."

Upstairs there are three bedrooms, the master has a beautiful en suite, with an egg-shaped tub that would fit both Chris and me. We head across the hall to the bedroom that faces the backyard. I stare out the window and feel him come up behind me. He wraps his arms around my waist. "Do you think Madison will like this room?"

I freeze and turn around. "What do you mean?" My heart beats frantically in my chest as I wait from him to speak.

"I mean this place is ours, I bought it for us." He smiles down at me.

Tears fill my eyes. "Oh my god," I cry. "I want to kiss you so hard but I can't."

"As soon as the oral surgeon gives us the go ahead, we'll come and christen every room." Chris tips my head back enough to lean down, kissing me softly on the lips.

"Promise?" I say with a pout.

He pulls me into a tight hug. "Come on, let me show you the rest."

Once we finish and we're back downstairs, I stop in front of the front door. "You want us to live here with you, right?"

"Of course, isn't it obvious?"

"I just wanted to double check. I was afraid I was dreaming, and it wasn't real." I throw my arms around him and hug him tight. "I can't believe we get to raise our daughter here. To think that you did a lot of the work makes it that much more special." I kiss him softly. "You gave me my teal door."

"Of course, baby. I'll give you whatever your heart desires."

I know he means it too, that's why in the foyer of our home I pull Chris to the floor and promptly show him how much I love him.

EPILOGUE

Chris
Five years later

$\mathcal{I}$ pull into the driveway and see the curtains move and smile. I hop out of my truck and pick up Madison's pink motorized Mini Cooper and stick it inside the open garage door. The minute I step inside, I find my little angel standing at the top of the stairs with her hands on her hips. "Daddy, the boys are making me mad."

"Come here, baby." I pick up my wife's miniature twin and kiss her cheek. "What did the boys do?"

These past five years have been the best of my life. I've been sober for a little over six years and I'm pretty fucking proud of myself. We moved into our home a month after I showed it to her. We got engaged six months after that.

The wedding took place in Haddie's parents' backyard. Natalie pulled Madison down the aisle in a wagon decorated in flowers. We kept it small, with just close friends and family.

My bride was beautiful in a simple white tank top maxi dress and flowers in her hair. I wore khakis and a white button up shirt. Abby was Haddie's matron of honor and Dad was my best man. At that point Joe and I were slowly working on our relationship, now we're better than ever.

We honeymooned in Cancun, since we didn't drink, we did lots of activities, ate a lot of good food, and made love every night.

Three years ago we found out that Haddie was pregnant, we weren't trying, but not preventing it. Imagine our surprise when we found out we were having twins, fraternal. My girl had the easiest pregnancy ever, and of course our payback from that, is the dynamic duo—our boys are crazy, and I mean that the best way possible.

Tucker, or as we call him Tank, is the oldest by five minutes, and certainly the ringleader. Xander is quieter, but just as destructive. They're all about their Momma.

Haddie is doing hospice homecare still, but now she's a trainer of the new staff and she loves it. Plus, she's no longer on call, but sometimes she will see patients for her co-workers.

Dad has started dating again. Gina, his girlfriend, is great and treats him well. She never gets upset when we talk about my mom, but I think it helps she's a widow as well. She loves my kids and they love her. Will they ever get married? I don't know, but I just want my dad to be happy.

I focus back on Madison. "What did the boys do?" We head upstairs to the boys' room.

"They stomped on my glitter crayons and now Momma is mad and saying dirty words while she cleans it up." I kiss her head, and when we reach the top, I poke my head in Madison's room to find my wife on the floor scrubbing.

Haddie sees me and shakes her head. "They're in time out."

I step into the room and she tips her head back, accepting my kiss. She's even more beautiful today. I married my best friend, and we've created this amazing life together. "I'll go check on them and I'll come back to help."

I step into the boys' room and find them sitting in chairs facing the opposite corners. Tank turns to look at me. "Daddy, we trouble."

"I heard, we don't step on sissy's glitter pen right?" They both nod. "Okay we're going to get sissy some new ones this weekend." They both get up and run to me. I scoop them up and kiss them both on the cheek. "Now let's go tell sissy sorry."

Haddie is coming out of the bedroom with Madison next to her. Once the boys apologize, we all head downstairs for dinner.

* * *

THE KIDS ARE all asleep and I kiss my wife to quiet her cries, before she wakes any of them up. I reach between us, rubbing her clit until I feel her pulsing around me as she comes all over my cock. I grab her leg and bring it up over my hip as I begin to pound into her. She takes everything I give to her, and when I feel those familiar tingles start I pick up the pace until I pump once, twice, and then three times inside of her.

She wraps her arms and legs around me and buries her face in my neck. I kiss her sweaty temple and sigh.

We may have started out rocky, but it led us to where we are now. I'll never regret any of it because I wouldn't have Haddie, Madison, or the boys if I hadn't done what I did.

"Chris, are you okay?"

I look down into Haddie's beautiful blue eyes. "I'm better than okay." I lean down and kiss her. "I love you, our babies, and the life we made. Thank you for always believing me."

Haddie pulls me down to her lips, kissing me with all she's got. It doesn't take long before I'm hard again, this time I roll us so she's on top. "Now I'm going to show you what you mean to me," she says right before she slides down my length and then does what she promised.

* * *

Ten years later

I STAND in front of the podium and look at the back of the room. My beautiful wife, my kids, Dad, mother and father-in-law, and my best friend/brother-in-law all smile at me. I clear my throat and keep eye contact with Haddie. Her smile is bright and encouraging. I look around at the people sitting. "Hi, I'm Chris, and I'm an alcoholic and an addict. I've been sober for sixteen and a half years." I then share my story, hoping to help at least one person.

THE END

NATIONAL INSTITUTE ON ALCOHOL
ABUSE AND ALCOHOLISM

If you or someone you know needs help:

National Institute on Alcohol Abuse and Alcoholism
www.niaaa.nih.gov
301–443–3860

NATIONAL INSTITUTE ON DRUG
ABUSE

WWW.NIDA.NIH.GOV

301–443–1124
National Institute of Mental Health
www.nimh.nih.gov
1–866–615–6464

ACKNOWLEDGMENTS

First of all, thank you to my husband for always supporting my dreams. He cleans and cooks when I'm on a deadline. He puts up with my crabbiness when I am on a deadline. His support means the world to me.

To my boys, thank you for not hating me when I have to put on the noise cancelling headphones

Thank you to my ARC team. Your continued support means everything to me. I hope you keep reading and keep reviewing. To Toni, thank you for editing this book and making it shine. To team Limitless, thank you for continuing to believe in me.

Lastly, to my readers. Thank you for always supporting me and joining me on his crazy journey. I love you guys so much and your never-ending support means so much to me.

BEFORE YOU GO…

DON'T MISS OUT!

Would you like to be a part of our *FREEBIE FRIDAY LIST* and get **6 FREE eBooks** and other *exclusive* sales sent to your inbox every Friday?

One email every week packed with bookish goodies!

We send out different genres such as Romance, Suspense, Thriller, Westerns, Paranormal, New Adult, and much more! If you'd like to join over 53,000+ subscribers, click below to be a part of FREEBIE FRIDAY…

Join FREEBIE FRIDAY!

BECOME A BOOKSHARK!

Who doesn't love a good eBook bargain?

Now, imagine receiving daily eBook sales straight to your inbox...*Bookworm heaven*!

Sign up for the ***BOOKSHARK NEWSLETTER*** and don't miss out on epic eBook sales ever again!

BECOME A BOOKSHARK

ABOUT THE AUTHOR

A Midwesterner and a readaholic most of my life until one day an idea came to me and a writing career was born. I'm a sucker for happily ever afters and love creating fictional worlds that others can get lost in. I love putting my characters through the ringer, but I love when they get to that satisfying, swoony ending.

When the voices give it a rest, which isn't often, I am usually found with my e-reader in her hand. Some of my favorites include Aurora Rose Reynolds, (the queen) Kristen Ashley, Kaylee Ryan, Natasha Madison, and Harper Sloan. I find a lot of my inspiration in music, movies, TV shows, and life.

I'm a wife to Jim and a mom to Ethan and (the real) Evan, a weightlifter, a medical scribe, college student and an author. How do I it? Rosé.

Facebook Reader Group

www.ingramcontent.com/pod-product-compliance
Lightning Source LLC
Chambersburg PA
CBHW031232260626
47169CB00007B/2265